MAGICAL MIDNIGHT

CATHERINE LANIGAN

Author of Angel Watch, Divine Nudges, Angel Tales, Romancing the Stone,
The Jewel of the Nile, The Christmas Star, The Sweetest Heart

CAT NOLAN PUBLISHING
LA PORTE, INDIANA
www.catherinelanigan.com

Library of Congress Cataloging-in-Publication Data

Copyright Catherine Lanigan 2023
Library of Congress #1-13089297931
ISBN: 979-8-218-96669-0

All rights reserved. Printed in the United States of America. No part of this publication may be reproduced, stored in a retrieval system or transmitted in any form or by any means, electronic, mechanical, photocopying, recording or otherwise, without the written permission of the publisher.

Publisher: Cat Nolan Publishing
             512 Andrew Avenue
             PO BOX 112
             La Porte, IN. 46350

"God bless us, every one!"

--- Charles Dickens
A Christmas Carol

One

THE OTHER SIDE/22nd DIMENSION/HEAVEN

She had lived forever.
Being an immortal carried a wealth of divine knowledge, galactic responsibilities and an undying compassion for all creatures and races created by All That Is.

Rhapsodically, Angel 7777 called her home heaven. But the scientific fact of the matter was that her existence and that of the other celestial beings like her existed in the 963 frequencies of the Creator. This dimension of being in the divine matrix was and is pure love. Within her realm, Angel 7777 could manifest and create just about anything. If she thought it, it came to fruition. She possessed a superior talent as an artist. Her creations held such a high vibration that her works became thought patterns that entered the minds and hearts of passionate light-being artists on many planets in several galaxies. On Venus, she was known as the Muse. Throughout the Andromeda Galaxy, she was called Divine Diva. She received countless calls for inspiration and assistance from other-world artists. Though she was in high demand, truly the first artist in heaven to be called upon for help, she was never power-hungry nor inflated—angels never tread those dark shadows. No point.

She thought she had fulfilled her loftiest purpose until one magical day.

That was the day she peered through her floating portal and connected with a human being.

Like any other time in timeless eternity, "eternal day" in heaven was filled with glorious music that wafted through Angel 7777's mind with joy and never-ending bliss. The sparkling glow of pulsating kaleidoscopic colors flowed through her entire being, her heart and out through her hands as she swooped her palm over a transparent holographic canvas. Her thoughts flowed like mercurial waters. Once the painting was finished, she telepathically sent the image to a favored artist on planet Sirius who was working on the interior of a new temple.

When she went back to work, her mind was a blank. Pure white. Blank. She closed her eyes, forcing the next image to appear. She put her fingers to her temples. She massaged her scalp and tossed back her blonde hair determined to find her own inspiration. Nothing came to mind. She stared at the colors around her, but they only blurred into shapeless blobs.

"What's happening to me?"

A small floating square portal appeared. Seldom had she needed to investigate the portal to other planets or galaxies for ideas. But this time was different. Something urged her to use the portal.

Peering into the portal she saw the familiar stargate tunnel shoot her focused mind across the dimensions. "Take me where I'm most needed," she urged telepathically to the portal.

That's odd. I've never thought that before. Am I needed somewhere in particular?

Stars zoomed past her mind's eye. Suddenly, the trajectory slowed as if it were moving in a thick gas; then it slowed more. White mists and clouds parted to reveal a dark night sky. It was if she had landed in another plane of existence.

"Oh, my heavens. Am I seeing Earth? Other angels have whispered about it, but I've never traveled here. How interesting." She looked closely at the vision that came into focus.

A large body of water, nearly a sea, glittered in moonlight. At first, Angel 7777 thought she was seeing the reflection of stars on the water, but then she realized that the stars were dangling in trees that lined the shore. "How beautiful. How creative!"

She immediately went to work manifesting a copy of the scene she saw through the portal onto her holographic canvas. The shapes and forms of the trees were magical, she thought, lit in the way that they were. Next to the trees she realized there was a wide boulevard where more lights appeared. But these lights were moving. She looked more closely.

To her left Angel B-2222 instantly appeared. "Those are headlights. On the cars."

"Cars."

"Automobiles. Humans use them to go places. They can't bilocate or teleport like we can."

Angel 7777 added the cars and headlights to her painting. "I can't imagine that." She glanced at Angel B-2222 whose long dark hair fell past her iridescent wings to her waist. She wore a white tunic exactly like Angel's with a gold rope at her waist and solid gold wing-shaped clips at the shoulders. The two angels were of the same rank. "You know a lot about earth?"

"I do. I watch them a great deal."

"Why? They seldom ask for my help."

"And they forget to thank us for the miracles we do perform. That's a pity."

Angel 7777 dropped her hands. "They don't believe in us anymore."

"Not so much."

Angel 7777 put her hands on either side of her portal and let her mind sink and sail through the wormhole, through the dimensions and to the place on earth that had chosen to show itself to her. "I wonder…."

CHICAGO. PRESENT TIME.

Owen Michaels, adjusted his silk tie as he sat in stalled traffic on Lake Shore Drive oblivious to the multitude of Christmas lights strung across skyscraper roofs, the trees along the lakeshore and in garlands in storefront windows. As he pulled up to the light at Grant Street Park, he didn't notice the group of picketers carrying signs protested UNFAIR WAGES. A few streets over was another rally with protestors shouting, "STOP LAKE POLLUTION", which nearly drowned out a Christmas song concerning a reindeer killing someone's grandmother coming from a department store loud speaker. As Owen hit the gas and crossed the intersection, he glanced briefly at the Salvation Army Santa who was being slugged in the jaw by a young man in a hoodie who then grabbed the red kettle and took off running.

Owen shook his head at the scene. He couldn't stop to save Santa. He was closing his biggest deal of the year on his Bluetooth.

But….

"Mr. Elsworth, could you hold on for a just a sec for me? Thanks." Owen put his client's call on hold and punched out 911. "Hello, I'd like to report a robbery in progress at Lake

Shore Drive near Grant Park. A man just stole Santa's red bucket."

"Thank you, sir. Yours is the third call. We're on it."

"Excellent," Owen replied and went back to his client. "Thanks for waiting, Mr. Elsworth. I'm pleased you liked the plan I executed for you, Mr. Elsworth. Your estate is secure. I'll get back to you after the holidays."

Owen exhaled a long Wim Hof breath of relief when he ended the call. Prudently, he used his turn signal as he turned his BMW to the left and was immediately cut off by a large SUV with the door bashed in. "Hey Buddy! Watch it!"

The driver gave Owen a dirty look and shook his fist at him as if Owen were in the wrong. "Merry Christmas to you, too," Owen said and continued on his way. He placed a call to his girlfriend, Julia, which was picked up immediately. Owen liked that she never left him hanging. Well, almost never. Sometimes. Okay. Seldom did she answer immediately.

"Julia, honey. I'm gonna be a bit late. I must make a stop."

Julia's voice was rushed and frustrated. It was almost as if she didn't want to take his call, he thought. "Owen, it—whatever it is, can wait. I need you here."

Owen swung the car into a parking garage, "No it can't wait." He had no more than finished his sentence when a car came screeching out of the garage and missed his front headlight by a millimeter. Owen's eyes scrunched shut. "Oh, God."

"What is it?" Julia asked. "Never mind. Just be here."

"I will. Promise." Owen ended the call, took his keys and shoving his arms in his cashmere overcoat, he got out of the car. Just as the attendant walked up to take his keys and give him his ticket, a family of five came up all of them overloaded with shopping bags and boxes. Two of the kids were squabbling and slapping each other, as they ran toward Owen as if he could save them---from something. Themselves? He thought. The parents were arguing about the money they'd spent and the toddler the mother carried was screaming at the top of his lungs.

As Owen walked away, he noticed that the parking attendant immediately got in the BMW and jerked his car up the interior drive, whisking his car and himself to safety away from the unhappy family.

Just as Owen walked through the revolving glass door to the department store, directly behind him a police officer chased a young man in a Bears jacket and jeans and who was brandishing a pistol. Owen doubled his steps to safety inside the brightly lit store.

The aisles were jam-packed with shoppers pushing and shoving. "What happened to on-line shopping?" he said aloud. A woman wearing a long puffy coat and severe black eye makeup obviously heard him and said, "There's no Christmas spirit on-line."

Owen shrugged his shoulders as he looked around for the fine jewelry counter. Weaving his way upstream through the clogged aisle, he finally made it to the lighted glass counter. He'd hoped for a possibly relaxing perusal of diamond earrings for Julia. Though today was his birthday, he'd always bought his mother, Kris, flowers or something meaningful on his birthday. His mother was still the most perfect person he'd ever known, but now that she had passed, his birthday didn't have the same uplifting emotions he once had. It wasn't the cake she baked from scratch or the silly cards she'd buy or the prettily wrapped clothes he needed desperately as he always outgrew them practically before they were out of the box. It was the loving words she put on the side of the store-bought card that took him away to that place in his childhood when he was the center of his parents' world. Where he could do no wrong and didn't want to do anything to betray his Dad's or Mom's trust and love in him. He owed them that. He never wanted his mother to look down from heaven and be displeased. That was why he worked himself to the top of the ladder on as a money manager. For eight years in a row, he'd won Manager of the Year for the entire Chicagoland area. That was saying something. Sometimes, he'd look at his awards and plaques and he could hear his mother tell him that she was proud of him.

Yes, he'd been a lucky kid. He had good upbringing. He wished that kind of happy childhood on all kids.

"Not that one! Can't you see where I'm pointing?" A brash, loud-mouthed woman who reeked of spending too much time at the perfume counter shouted at the obviously over-tired young woman behind the counter.

"I'm so sorry, ma'am," the jewelry attendant apologized. "This one?" She picked up another box.

"Yes. Finally." The woman inspected the necklace.

"I'll be right with you," the attendant said to Owen.

"No, you're serving me now. And this won't do. Let me see the green stones."

"Emeralds," the young woman winked at Owen.

Owen returned the wink and said softly, "I'll take those large diamond hoop earrings. Here's my credit card. I'll be back."

Thank you, the attendant mouthed. "I'll gift wrap them personally for you, sir," the attendant replied gratefully.

Owen went to the escalator and was nearly knocked off by an obese man who pushed his way ahead of Owen. The man lost his footing and started to fall backward onto Owen. Owen's hands shot out to help hold the man up and keep his balance.

"Take your hands off me!" The obese man shouted and beat at Owen's hands.

"I was just…."

"What? Trying to help me? Or kill me?"

Owen closed his gaping mouth. Replying to insanity was a waste of time.

As the escalator reached the second floor, Owen saw that it was even more crowded than the streetside floor. He worked his way over to the men's parkas. He flipped through the rack, chose a warm looking coat with a hood and zip out lining. He went to the counter and paid cash for the coat.

"Can you ship it to this address? It's for my Dad."

"Certainly sir. Would you like it gift wrapped?"

"Sure."

Owen finished his transaction and as he put his wallet away, his cell phone rang. Looking at the caller ID, he bumped into an elderly woman.

"Watch it!" She growled.

"I wasn't…."

"Pervert!" She bit back and walked away talking to herself.

Owen went back to his call as he got on the down escalator. "Hello, Dad."

OTHER SIDE/ HEAVEN.

Angel 7777 felt a rustle by her side. Angel B-2222 was now looking into the portal with her.

"What are you seeing that has your attention?" Angel B-2222 asked.

"I'm not quite sure. I thought this was Christmas time on earth."

"It is," Angel B-2222 agreed.

"Then I'm not seeing earth. Something is wrong here."

"Change the location. See what else there is. You know—get the whole picture."

Angel 7777 smiled. "I will." She spread her fingers over the portal as it enlarged to encompass an entirely different scene. Gone was the city and instead she saw the setting sun over a snow-covered high hill in majestic pastoral land. In the distance was a white painted cow barn, a milking Parlor, calf hutches and a farm house with a front porch festooned with lighted evergreen garlands and red ribbons. Along the edge of the high hill was a row of pine trees, conifers and blue spruces. An old tractor with an attached wagon was parked near the row of trees.

In the tractor's driver seat was Gregory Michaels. Some things, Angels knew about humans upon first encounters. Such as Angel 7777 knowing Gregory was seventy-five years old. He was over six foot tall and still muscular from a lifetime of farm work. He was a hard working man, with love and respect for nature.

Angel 7777 felt his strong energy and high frequency instantly. Loving hearts did that to her.

In the wagon was a bundled evergreen tree, a Golden Retriever and three "transparent" spirits. Gregory's parents, David and Penny Michaels had left the earth decades ago in earth years. They were now back to their young, healthy twenty-five year-old bodies. They were dressed in their favorite 1950's attire that they both dearly loved.

Angel 7777 turn to Angel B-2222. "I know them! I've seen them here."

"So, have I. Good people. I like them. They dance a lot and bring joy to everyone who knows them." She smiled happily as a tinkling vibrational sound resonated.

"They're Gregory's parents. Owen's grandparents. Then that beautiful woman must be Owen's mother, Kris. She's young again, as well. That's what I love about where we live. Everyone is healthy and so happy."

"I like her hair. It is styled after that actress we met. Farrah."

"Lovely soul." Angel 7777 looked closer at the scene as Beau, the Golden Retriever, barked at the three "spirits". "Dogs see everything. Too bad humans cannot communicate with dogs. Hmm. This is getting interesting."

BLACK RIVER, WISCONSIN

Gregory used a strong hemp rope to finish securing the tree to the wagon sides. Though a wind picked up as the sun set, David's ducktail hair did not move, nor did Penny's full poodle skirt. Beau barked again at the spirits.

"Thanks, Mom. Thanks, Dad. Christmas is the most special time of year. You taught me that and Kris, my only love, you and I kept that going for Owen all his life. Didn't we? He was the apple of your eye. Mine, too." Gregory ruffled Beau's ears and put his nose next to Beau's. "And this year, Owen will be home for Christmas. It doesn't get any better than that."

"We agree!" The trio of spirits chimed.

Beau barked.

"Hush, Beau. They're family. They're here to help with Christmas and don't you tell. People will think I'm nuts—seeing dead people."

Gregory punched his cell phone. "Owen? Can you hear me?'

"Dad?" Owen answered.

"Happy Birthday, son!" Gregory smiled at Beau as he hopped onto the tractor's driver seat and Beau took his co-pilot position on the floor.

"You remembered!" Owen was surprised.

"I've never forgotten and your mother is---"

"Smiling down from heaven," Owen finished.

"Your mom always smiles at us, son. Guess what? I just cut down that conifer we planted when you were what? Six? Eight years-old?"

"Six. A long time ago."

"I know. I know. It all goes too fast for me, Owen." Gregory touched his eye, cleared the emotion from his throat and asked, "So, did you get your client's plan all wrapped up?"

"I did."

"Fantastic! We can celebrate that, too, when you come home for Christmas."

"Uh, Dad. We talked about this. Julia is designing the Yacht Club gala for Christmas Eve. I promised her I'd be there."

"Julia. Again. Uh, so, hey! Here's an idea. Why don't the both of you come up on Christmas Day? I bought a twenty-pound turkey. Plenty for all!"

"Dad, her parents are having a big brunch the next day at their house. You should see this mansion. Forty people and a lot of them could be potential clients for me in the New Year. You understand."

Gregory held a hand over his heart as his chin dropped to his chest. He shook his head. But the pain of disappointment rang through his body like funeral bells. "Sure, son. Maybe next year."

"Glad you understand, Dad. I'll call you on Christmas."

Gregory's hand shook as he tapped the iPhone to end the call. He looked up to the stars wondering if there was any hope for him.

"Last year it was Amanda. Now—Julia. This year I was hoping it would be me---and home."

He held his breath as Beau laid his head on Gregory's thigh. Joy left Gregory as he exhaled into the icy December night. "Do you still make miracles up there?"

* * * * *

Two

THE OTHER SIDE/HEAVEN.

Angel 7777's attention was so focused on Gregory's disappointment; she didn't hear Angel B-2222 talking to her. Her friend's telepathic thoughts buzzed in her message receptacles, but Gregory's sorrow was almost overwhelming. Her act of curiosity had led her down this path and now she was determined to understand more about this human family and the mysteries of their need to control their innate need for love.

"You need to come away from the portal," Angel B-2222 said again.

"No, I don't. I want to understand more fully. Perhaps these emotions of theirs are something I can capture in my painting."

"We understand love to the greatest degree…we live love through all eternity."

"This man just asked me for help. I know he could feel me watching him."

Angel B-2222's wings raised on her back, a sure sign of conflict about to rise. "You're treading…"

"I know…where I'm not allowed. But, the rule is, that if a human asks for help, then I'm compelled, ordered actually to help."

"Fine. So pray for him."

Angel 7777. "I will. Just as soon as I know what exactly that prayer should be." She felt a new sensation. A searing fierceness jolted through her being. She'd learned from one of the archangels that this kind of energy was called determination. Was she being elevated to a new status? Perhaps she'd entered that energy band the warrior angels referred to as courage. Her energy centers felt as if she'd been set on fire. Clearly, something was happening now that was more than just her curiosity. Or was she being the fool angel as her friend, Angel B-2222 feared?

Then as if reading her mind, Angel B-2222 said, "Your curiosity will be your downfall, Angel 7777."

"You could use a bit more of it," Angel 7777 chuckled as she turned back to peer into the portal. The scene on earth cleared. "Oh! There he is! It's Owen again."

CHICAGO. PRESENT DAY.

As Owen drove up to the Chicago Yacht Club, he couldn't help but be intimidated by the fact that Julia's family, the Whitehouses, had been founding fathers of the club since

1875. They were wealthy, that was true, but it was the weight of the family name and connections that was more trusted than gold. At least in Chicago. Julia adored sailing as did just about every member of her family. Owen had never been on a boat until last summer and one sailing trip with the Whitehouses and their friends to Mackinac Island was all it took for him to realize that his farm life background, Masters in Finance from University of Chicago and his position as the youngest Vice-President at a boutique financial firm had limited his vision, scope and goals in life. He saw Julia and the world in which she moved as an event planner and designer for influential and power magnates in the mid-west as the key to his future. And bonus, she appeared to love him.

He fingered the small box holding the diamond earrings. "Possibly love me."

He pulled the car up the drive noticing the evergreen trees were artistically woven with a massive number of blue and white crystal lights. He'd met Julia's lighting crew the previous week. They were masters of their work. And in high demand. "Not like stringing lights back on the farm," he mumbled as he pulled to a stop at the club entrance.

Two valets were on duty. The youngest one, dashed toward Owen as he opened the door.

"Good evening, Mr. Michaels," he said jovially. "Miss Whitehouse is in the dining room." He leaned closer. "She's been here all day."

"Really? Then she's ready for a break."

As Owen walked around the car, he noticed a Salvation Army Volunteer in Uniform and with his red collection bucket dangling from the tripod. Owen pulled out his wallet. Because he'd just paid cash for his dad's parka, only a single dollar bill was left. He felt ridiculous gifting only a dollar, but the volunteer smiled generously.

"Merry Christmas, Sir."

Owen smiled. "Merry...."

He was interrupted by his cell phone ringing. Frowning, he said, "Dad. Don't try to guilt me into coming there." Owen walked with long strides into the dining room and halted.

Though the lake and night lights were always stunning through the wide expanse of windows, the room was decorated in garlands filled with silver and blue feathers, crystal icicles and snowflakes and twinkling white lights. The tables were draped in blue cloths, silver napkins, elegant white bone china with silver rims and crystal water and wine glasses. Three-foot-tall crystal vases held cascades of white roses, spruce and eucalyptus greenery, blue feathers and teardrop crystal prisms.

Julia stood in the middle of the room dressed in a winter white knit dress that fit her slim, shapely body like a glove. Her blonde hair was clipped at the nape, but the escaping tendrils testified to her frazzled mood.

"Dad," Owen began.

"I'm just saying, son, that I'd like to see you is all."

"I get it."

Julia turned as she heard Owen's voice. He waved at her. Without a smile, she snapped her fingers and gestured for him to come to her side.

Owen blinked.

An Asian woman about thirty years of age with voluminous long black hair and dressed in a black wool dress and designer high heeled red shoes spoke to Julia. Julia wasn't listening to the woman, she was occupied with commanding Owen. He couldn't tell if she wanted him to rescue her from the woman or if she was angry with him. Either way, Julia clearly was not happy now. He'd hoped for a better reception--it being his birthday.

"Dad. Let me call you tomorrow. I'm in the middle of something."

"Tomorrow," Gregory responded lowly as he hung up.

Owen put his cell in his jacket pocket and walked over to Julia. She bussed his cheek.

Not a good sign. He thought.

"You're late."

"You're busy," he retorted.

"This is a nightmare. Every delivery was late. The colors are all wrong. Everything is ---off."

Owen looked around at the stunning room, "Yeah, no Santa or candy canes."

"Honestly, Owen. You can be uber-tacky. These feathers are supposed to be midnight blue. Not this royal blue."

"Sorry."

"You don't see it?"

"Uh, no. They're blue."

"Ugh! Owen. You're so…"

"What?" He smiled flirtatiously.

Julia's mood broke. She leaned over and kissed him. "You are totally what I need to get out of myself."

"Yeah?" he put his arms around her and pulled her close. "So, let's blow this pop stand and go have dinner."

"Sure. Let me wrap up."

Julia gave him another kiss before leaving his arms. As she walked over to her crew, Owen rocked back on his heels and whispered to himself, "Maybe a good birthday after all."

Julia walked over to the Asian woman who was working on an enormous flower arrangement.

"Cynthia, this is all wrong."

"It's Chantal," the woman answered through pursed lips as if this had happened prior.

"Right. Sorry. I'm bad at names."

"I noticed." She paused giving Julia a hard stare. "I followed your instructions."

Chantal picked up a photograph of a floral arrangement and handed it to Julia.

"Oh, no. This is wrong. I updated this a week ago. Good Lord, can't anyone do anything right around here?"

Owen glanced at the crew still hanging garlands who all rolled their eyes and shook their heads. Clearly, they would not be the first to volunteer to work with Julia again. Owen watched as Julia went to another table and took a manila folder over to Chantal.

"This is what I need."

Chantal pulled out the photograph. Her eyebrows raised in dismay. "Okay." She forced a smile. "Snowflakes and rhinestones. I'm on it."

"Excellent."

Julia immediately spun around and swooped back to Owen, thrust her arm through his.

"I'll check on them after dinner."

"After? I---thought we'd go dancing after dinner. This being…"

"Owen," Julia interrupted. "This gala is killer for me. It's the first time Lola has trusted me as lead designer. Of course, she saddled me with a virgin crew and two interns to boot."

Owen tried to buoy up his mood. "Well, okay. No dancing. I made reservations at La Grille. Nothing but the best for my baby."

"Sweetie, I cannot. All my parents' friends will be at the gala. Important people for your future." She placed her palm over his chest. "I'm doing this for us."

Owen didn't feel the "us" in any of what she said or was doing. In fact, he was just about as deflated as he could feel. It was odd. He'd just closed the biggest deal of the year. And it was...

"Julia. Did you forget? It's —"

She interrupted again. "What?" She harrumphed. "Christmas? Fairy tales and silliness. I'm beyond that," she said as they walked out of the ballroom.

Owen turned around and waved an arm at the crew inside. "Thanks for a great job, guys!"

The older man on the ladder holding a thick swath of spruce and cedar greens, gave Owen a thumbs up and a wide smile. The Asian woman beamed.

It was amazing to Owen how a few simple words could make a room light up more than electric lights.

"Tell you what, Owen. Let's grab a burger in the bar and then I won't miss any time away from the job." She let go of his arm and walked ahead of him.

"Sure. And happy birthday to me."

* * * * *

The Deco North Lake Shore Apartment Buildings were built in 1927. Then and now their view of Lake Michigan was considered supreme among Chicagoans. The combination of Art Deco, history, attention to detail and the contemporary renovations were everything that Owen wanted and dreamed of for his living quarters. He was within walking distance to just about anything and everything he needed. Restaurants, theaters. His office on Wabash Street.

He'd been lucky to snag one of the premium apartments that offered a lake view. That had been a chance lunch with Julia's father, Ernest, whose business partner died that afternoon. Ernest informed Owen that the apartment at Deco North Lake Shore would come available. Owen asked for an introduction to the deceased family.

Ernest did better than that. He called the family attorney and put Owen's name in on a bid list for the apartment. Then Julia pressured her father to do more. She told her father that Owen's address was important to his future as a financial manager among their friends. Ernest agreed.   Thanks to Julia and Ernest, no other bidders were taken and Owen won the apartment by the next morning.

It had all happened so fast, Owen had barely time to think, pack and move. He'd paid a high ticket for it, but the night sky was important to him. He'd always been drawn to star gazing, he thought, as he walked into his one-bedroom apartment and hung up his coat.

"Yep. Ever since Dad gave me that telescope when I was eight. Yeah. That was a good Christmas."

He looked around the small room. No Christmas tree. No garlands, lights or wrapped presents. "Not even one of Julia's wrong blue feathers," he joked to himself. "Well, I've been busy." He glanced at the small dining table filled with files, his laptop and unopened mail. The windows were devoid of drapes and the wooden slat blinds were drawn up so that he could see every inch of Lake Michigan and sky.

It was a clear night. Not a cloud in the sky. Stars blinked at him. "I wonder what the galaxies would look like from a space ship," he mused as he used the remote control to turn on the satellite radio.

Frank Sinatra's voice crooned "I'll Be Home for Christmas."

"Who requested that? My dad?"

Going to the kitchen, he opened a bottle of red wine, poured himself a glass, went back to the living room and sat down in an overstuffed leather chair where he could look out over the lake and up to the stars. Owen was always amazed at the massive size of Lake Michigan. He called it "the Michigan Sea." It was four times the size of the United Kingdom and archeologists had found Stonehenge-like rock arrangements in the depths of the lake.

Odd, he thought. Factoids like that came from his mother. She often said, "Every day was an opportunity to learn something new."

Still listening to the music, his hand rested on the small table next to the chair where a framed photograph of his mother sat. "Mom."

He rubbed his forehead hoping to ease the sudden pounding he felt. It didn't work. The pounding and pain continued. He rested his head on the back of the chair. "I miss you, Mom."

He looked up to the stars as the pain in his head fell to his throat, where it burned. It was his birthday. His mother had called him her "almost Christmas baby." She'd told him he was special and he was –to her.

His eyes burned, but he would not let tears come.

He didn't get it. He should be on top of the world, yet even his to-die-for small apartment wasn't a real home. It was a place to hang his hat until--- "Until what, Owen?"

Until his life began? And what was that? He had money, position, the most beautiful girlfriend in Chicago from an historic Lake Shore family. Yet he felt as if he was tumbling down a rabbit hole to an abyss.

Had it all gone blank when his mother died? Or was that an excuse for what he was searching for? Wasn't his work meaningful enough? He was helping people who had no clue about finances, take charge of their future for themselves and their legacies.

Even his boss told him he was at the top of his game. But his enormous business deal closing felt empty to him. Scenes of his afternoon Christmas shopping flew across his mind. Julia and her upscale Christmas party. His lackluster birthday. He felt in his pocket. The diamond earrings were still there. He didn't feel like gift giving. He didn't feel the Christmas spirit. He felt numb.

"Christmas means nothing anymore."

* * * * *

Three

THE OTHER SIDE/HEAVEN.

Angel 7777's eyes held onto Owen's eyes as he looked through the stars, through the dimensions and straight into the 963 hertz frequency where Angel existed. She knew she was seeing and experiencing his soul. It was unlike any feeling-- any vibrations she had ever felt. His compassion met hers like a magnate. It was pushing and pulling at the same time. She felt the energy field around her shake as his heartfelt prayer hit her.

Instantly, her hands flew away from the portal and she was blown back.

An even stranger reaction was that she felt something warm, not unlike love, fill her eyes and then a particle rolled down her face.

"What are you doing?" Angel B-2222 asked.

"I don't know."

"I'll tell you what it is. That thing on your face is a tear. And Angels don't cry. Unless…"

"What?"

"You're greatly moved. Is it your painting? Your talent is impeccable."

"No, it's not. I can do better. Watch." Angel 7777 moved her hand over her painting and transformed it into an Impressionist spring scene.

"It's glorious."

"Manet thought so. But its not enough. I'm capable of more. I know how Owen down there on earth feels."

"You shouldn't have invaded his thoughts like that."

Angel 7777's wings started to unfurl in protest. Then she re balanced herself. "But I did and I learned that I'm not using my gifts to their fullest."

"What gifts would that be?"

"I should be helping the Universe."

Angel B-2222 put her hand on her hip. "Oh, for heaven's sake. We all do our best."

"Maybe you do. But I'm not so sure."

The atmosphere was suddenly filled with angelic humming and the tinkling sound of cherub laughter as the area above Angel 7777 and Angel B-2222 filled with a pulsing orb of rainbow light. It whirled in a clockwise motion and then undulated underneath itself and formed a counter-clockwise swirl of opalescent colors wrapped in liquid gold light.

From inside the swirl came an imperious deep voice that Angel 7777 had never encountered.

Angel B-2222 stiffened. "Uh, oh."

"What is it?"

"We're in for it now," Angel B-2222 warned.

The Imperious Voice boomed, "Angel 7777."

The orb hovered just over Angel 7777 as she straightened to attention. "Yes, sir?"

"What are you painting that displeases you?" The Imperious Voice inquired.

"Sir, it's not my work. It's the people that concern me," she answered.

"What people?"

"One person, really."

"Oh?"

"I can show you." She moved her hand over the square portal that revealed Owen Michael's life. He was still sitting in his chair looking at the night sky.

"Christmas means nothing anymore," Owen said.

Angel 7777 looked at the rainbow orb. "See what I mean? He's sad."

The booming voice answered, "I know about Owen. Now look at the others."

Angel 7777 whisked her hand over the portal. The city streets of Chicago were filled with people bickering. A man shot another with a gun. Thieves shoved an elderly woman and stole her purse. She fell to the pavement in pain. No one helped her. Angry vibrations of such a low frequency Angel 7777 knew they'd be trapped in hatred. Both were the food for evil.

Angel B-2222 looked from Angel 7777 to the Orb. "That was frightening."

"Yes," the Imperious Voice replied. "Just like Owen, all these others have…"

Angel 7777 interrupted, "Lost their faith."

"Yes, they have," the Imperious Voice said.

"Something needs to be done. I wish I could help."

Angel B-2222 shook her head vigorously at Angel 7777. "Don't…."

"You can!" The Imperious Voice boomed and the colors swirled around the two angels.

"I'm only one angel. Not to mention humans think we are myths," Angel 7777 countered.

"You can change that."

"How?" she asked.

The Imperious Voice grew louder. "The Law of the Universe decrees that the good faith of one act of kindness affects the collective."

Angel B-2222 took a step back away from the circle of the rainbow light. "Uh, oh."

"I know this law," Angel 7777 said.

"Me, too," Angel B-2222 added.

"Of course, you do. Both of you."

"I've never been to earth, but I've heard stories of other Angels who went there. It's very different."

"That it is," the Imperious Voice agreed.

Angel B-2222 touched Angel 7777's wing. "Angel---hush!"

"And difficult, I understand." She looked over at the portal again and into Owen's despondent face. "If he truly loses his faith, he won't have hope. And without hope---"

"He will lose his will to live," the Imperious Voice gave the warning.

"I DO have to help."

Angel B-2222's wings drooped. "Your open heart gets you into trouble every time."

"Hush, Angel B-2222. Sir? I meant it. Count me committed."

Angel B-2222 slapped her own forehead. "Oy."

"Angel 7777, The Council of Celestial Light of Twenty-Four believes you are up to the task."

"Then you'll send me?"

"It is done." Without another word or sound, the orb, the rainbow lights, the music and the Imperious Voice vanished.

Angel B-2222 looked at her friend. "I will pray for you. You'll need lots."

Angel 7777 smiled brightly. "I'll be fine. I will."

Angel was proud of herself. She had made the right decision. After all, goodness always triumphed over evil. Or so she'd been told.

* * * * *

Four

BLACK RIVER, WISCONSIN.

Gregory was proud of himself for all he'd done this December getting the house decorated to the max the way that Kris always did when she was alive. Though he'd bought the fresh pine wreath at the grocery store rather than make it from the cedar, pines and spruce branches on the farm the way Kris had, he actually had made a big red bow for it and added some battery operated lights which he thought was a merry addition.

He had wrapped the porch pillars in ten-year-old artificial garlands he'd found in the attic and added red ribbon to those. A bowl of nuts sat next to the Nutcracker soldier that Owen used to use to crack walnuts for Kris's Christmas cookies. He'd hung Owen's old Christmas stocking on the fireplace mantle, which was crowded with framed photos of Owen, Kris, David and Penny—all the people he loved.

"But he won't be coming home," he mumbled to himself as he tightened the last bolt into the tree trunk. He gave it one last crank and felt the screw twist further into the trunk.

"That ought to do it." Wiggling his way out from under the tree, he felt a twinge in his hand. "Musta wrenched my fingers tightening that trunk."

Slowly, he sat up, wiped the perspiration from his forehead and then rose. Though a bit wobbly on his feet, he managed to open the box with neatly packed multi-colored lights. Taking out the first string, he plugged them into the power surge bar on the floor. He strung the lights on the bottom first and worked his way up the tree.

He went to the kitchen to retrieve a step stool to reach the very top and when he came back into the living room, Beau was standing at attention on the other side of the sofa, wagging his tail.

"What is it, Beau?"

Gregory glanced at the sofa and there sat Kris in her bell bottom jeans, David and Penny, smiles of approval on their transparent faces.

"It's just beautiful, dear," Kris said telepathically. "The best tree ever."

"It's not even decorated yet," Greg replied.

"That was my job. You did the lights. Owen and I decorated the tree."

Greg put his hand on his heart. "Oh, how I wish you were alive so I could hug you."

"I'll always be in your heart," she said.

David gave Gregory a thumbs up. "Your mother and me, too, son."

"Thanks, Dad. Okay. Now for the Christmas Star."

Gregory stepped off the step-stool and reached over to the black and white Buffalo check upholstered chair where he'd placed the glass and brass five-pointed star. "I hope it still lights," he said, getting on the step-stool and reaching for the top center branch to anchor the star. He plugged the star into the last string of lights connector and it illuminated instantly.

"Oh, good job, son!" David applauded.

"It never ceases to take my breath away," Penny said.

Kris only stared long and hard at Gregory who had just retracted his left arm as if he's stuck it in an electrical socket.

"Oh, God!" Gregory groaned as he stumbled, righted himself long enough to back off the step-stool. Another searing pain shot through his chest. He grabbed his heart, sank to his knees. His eyes rolled in his head as the pain took him over.

He fell onto the floor.

"I have to help him. Do something!" Kris yelled.

Kris rushed to Gregory and put her hand on his arm, but it passed through him.

David and Penny watched with compassion, but they didn't move.

"There's nothing we can do. Nothing you can do, Kris. We're not human anymore."

* * * * *

CHICAGO.

Owen's wine glass was still full when his cell phone rang. He looked at the caller ID. "Relentless." He punched the screen. "Look, Dad—"

"Owen?" a woman's voice asked.

"Hello? Who is this?"

"It's Holly Kane. You haven't met me, but my husband and I work for your dad here on the farm. We live next door."

"That's nice. So, has he recruited you, too?"

"Recruited?"

"Never mind. So, why are you calling me on my dad's phone?"

"I came over to bring him a casserole for dinner and that's when I found him."

Owen bolted to his feet. "FOUND him?"

"Yes. Your dad had a heart attack while he was putting up the Christmas tree. He's so excited about your coming home. He's told us so much about you."

"Holly," Owen said raking his hand through his hair. "My dad…"

"He was on the floor. He'd been decorating the tree. I called 911 immediately, of course."

Owen felt his stomach turn to ice and his blood stop running. "Is he…still alive?"

"Yes, Owen. I'm so sorry. Yes. Yes. He's alive. The ambulance is here now. They'll take him to the hospital. I'll follow in my car and stay with him till you get here. My husband, Sam, will stay with our kids, so it's all okay."

"Oh, kids. Yeah," Owen looked around his living room as if he didn't know where he was. In one phone call his world had turned black, thick, and made no sense. That was it. He couldn't think. The impossible had just happened. His father was in perfect health. Owen knew that for certain because when he asked his father how he was doing; how was his health, Gregory always answered, "Healthy as a horse, son. You know me."

Yeah. He knew his proud, independent, stubborn, helicopter dad. Owen could have kicked himself. His dad was seventy-five. Not fifty-five or forty-five. Though he always acted young. And thought young. He wasn't. And now he'd had a heart attack.

"Okay. Okay. Holly, is it?"

"Yes. Owen."

"I'm on my way. It'll take several hours to get to Black River. I...I. Uh, when you see him, tell him I'm coming. Please."

"Of course. Black River Memorial Hospital. And Owen. Take your time. Pack a bag. He may need your care for several days. Weeks."

"Weeks? Oh, God. Listen, Holly. Thank you. Uh. Keep his phone so we can stay in touch while I'm on the road."

"I know this is a shock, Owen. But we are all praying for him. And besides, Christmas always brings miracles now, doesn't it?"

"Right. Bye for now."

Owen hung up, raked his hair, and tried to calm his brain into logical and strategic thoughts. "Weeks. How bad is it?" He wiped his face with his palms. "Buck up, Owen. He is going to pull through. You must do this."

Owen went to the hall closet and took out a small suitcase. "Weeks." He shook his head. He grabbed a hanging bag and his briefcase. He went to the table and packed his laptop, files, charging cords and iPad.

In the bedroom, he grabbed underwear, sweaters, jeans, socks and shoved them in his suitcase. From the bathroom he gathered his toiletries, razor, and toothbrush. He rushed back to the living room, snapped his fingers, and went to a drawer in the end table and took out his checkbook. He put it in his jacket pocket. "Weeks."

Gathering up his suitcase, hanging bag and briefcase he started for the door. He took one last look at the stars. One particular star appeared abnormally bright. Nearly like a super nova. Owen had studied stars off and on for years. He'd never seen anything like it. He didn't believe in "signs" like others did. He didn't have any kind of mystical streak in him that bent him to believe in prophesies or oracles. He was sensible and pragmatic. But as he stared at the too-brilliant star, he felt chills race down his spine and the hairs on the back of his neck stood on end.

"Don't you die on me, Dad."

* * * * *

It was after midnight when Owen arrived at Black River Memorial Hospital. After parking his car he went through the emergency room doors as all other doors to the hospital were locked. So Holly had informed him.

The skeleton staff and the sleeping patients gave a haunting and eerie feeling to the halls as Owen fast-walked past a lighted artificial Christmas tree and up to the reception desk. A chubby, blonde male nurse in his mid-forties was working on the computer and drinking a very tall vending machine coffee, according to the advertisement on the paper cup.

"Hello," Owen said to the nurse who slowly tore his eyes away from the computer screen.

"Hi. How can I help you?"

"My dad was brought in earlier. I called from the car…"

The man burst into a smile. "Oh, you must be Greg's son!" He rose from his chair and thrust his hairy arms and big hands out to shake Owen's hand. "Great guy, Greg. What a shame."

"Shame?"

"Oh, to have to be in a hospital at Christmas. He's been so excited to have you home for the holiday."

"So, you know him?"

"Lands, yes. I met him down at the Co-Op. My dad's a dairy farmer, too."

"Ah!" Owen's eyebrows shot up. "Guess the farm thing wasn't your gig, either."

"Oh, I do both. Have to help family when we can. Right?" The man smiled.

Doesn't he make me feel like a jerk? "So, what room is he in?"

"ICU."

"Oh my God." Owen wiped his forehead. "What condition is he in?"

"He's stable."

"Stable? Is that good? I mean, I can't believe this has happened. Then Christmas. I have a mountain of work before year's end. My girlfriend's gala…." Owen felt as if his head would burst.

"I know. It would make life easier if we could plan for these things, but that's not how it works. Life, I mean," he said.

Owen inhaled deeply to calm himself and looked around. "So, where do I go?"

The male nurse pointed down the hall. "The bank of elevators down this hall. He's on the fourth floor. A-1."

"Got it. Thanks."

"And Owen. Tell Greg that Jacob will be up to see him when my shift ends."

Owen gave Jacob a thumbs up and headed quickly for the elevators. He punched the button, the doors opened immediately and he got in.

Owen had never been in an ICU unit. In fact, he'd never been in a hospital but once. His mother had died at home. And the only time he'd come to this hospital was when Johnny Ames had broken his arm playing baseball and Gregory had driven Johnny to the hospital to get his cast put on.

He was surprised that all the doors to the rooms were open and each room was glassed in. He guessed immediately that the nurses and doctors could watch the critical patients more closely through glass walls.

When Owen walked toward Room A-1 he saw Greg sitting up in the bed, sound asleep but with so many tubes, wires and machines attached to him, he looked like a lead player in a Sci-Fi movie. The scene was shocking and scared the hell out of him.

"Hi," Owen said sheepishly to the pretty, blonde woman sitting in the chair next to his father. She wore a Christmas sweater, jeans, cowboy boots and little makeup. In her lap was a book. "You must be Holly."

"Guilty. Glad you made it, Owen," she said sweetly. She held up the book. "I was reading A Christmas Carol to him. I read it to my kids every Christmas. It's the craziest thing. They love the ghost stories."

"Ghosts. At Christmas," he replied not taking his eyes from his father. "He's pretty gray, isn't he?"

"Yes."

"How is he? Did the doctor say?"

"He's going to be fine. The doctor said it was a mild heart attack."

For the first time since Holly's call, Owen felt a genuine sigh of relief. "Oh, that's so good. So very good."

"Yes, it is," she smiled.

"So, what does that mean, exactly? A mild heart attack?"

She rose from the chair, closing her book. "The doctor said he'd be back about seven in the morning. He's done well all night. He may even be able to go home tomorrow, if his tests are good."

Owen's eyes widened. "Oh, my gosh! That's incredible."

She picked up her coat and walked over to Owen. She put her hand on his arm. He looked at it. People didn't usually touch him like that. It reminded him of something his mother used to do. He'd forgotten.

Holly dropped her hand. "This must be such a shock to you, Owen."

"Yeah. It was."

"Well, I'll be going. Sam and I will get the cows to the milking parlor in the morning. Don't you worry."

"Sam?"

"I told you. My husband."

"Oh, yes. I remember now. The milking. I forgot that, too."

"I'll see you tomorrow," she said.

"Holly. Thank you for staying with him. I'm sure it made a difference to have you here."

"I hope this isn't too strange for me to say this, but we're like family to Greg. He's been great with the kids. Letting them work on the farm and learn things. He's a good teacher. So patient with them."

"Bye, Owen." Holly walked away.

Owen turned around and walked over to his father whose shallow breaths barely made a sound. He touched his father's arm, observing the pick line and the saline drip he was hooked up to. The heart monitor beeped incessantly as the green graphic lines jumped across the screen. A canella was positioned in Greg's nostrils distributing an accurate flow of oxygen to his lungs.

It amazed Owen all the science, mechanics, and knowledge it took to keep a person alive when the body began to shut down. His father had been lucky that Holly found him when she did. He had been lucky that the farm was not too many miles from the hospital.

Luck was on his side as well. If his father was allowed to leave the hospital and go home, then Owen could get back to the city and his life.

Yes. They'd all been lucky.

* * * * *

Five

"**G**ood morning, all!" A cheery, masculine voice aroused Owen from the deepest sleep he'd experienced in years. Because he'd fallen asleep sitting in a chair, his neck felt as if it were permanently cricked in a lopsided position that his fitness gym masseuse would never return to normal. Holding his palm at the side of his neck, Owen rose from the uncomfortable chair to greet the grey haired, fit-looking sixty-ish man in a white lab coat.

He held out his hand to Owen. "I'm Doctor Ellis. You must be Owen."

"I am," Owen replied running his tongue over his dry lips. "Sorry. It was a long drive last night."

A dark-haired Indian looking woman was taking Greg's vitals. She peeled off the blood pressure cuff and nodded at Doctor Ellis. "One twenty over eighty-four."

Gregory beamed at Owen. "See, Owen? You brought me back to life."

Owen peered at his father who looked truly in the pink this morning as the nurse swept a digital thermometer over Gregory's forehead.

"Normal," she announced.

"And my other tests, Doc?" Gregory asked looking extraordinarily jolly. "Give it to me straight."

"Your tests were all good. Your cholesterol is high as you and I have discussed in the past. I'm putting you on a blood thinner. And I want to see you again in three days."

"So, I can go home?" Gregory asked.

"As long as Owen is here to watch you for a few days, that would be fine," Doctor Ellis said.

Owen looked from Doctor Ellis to his father and back again. "If he can go home, I really need to get back to my job."

"Owen, I don't want to stay here. Please."

"Dad. I have obligations." He nearly bit his tongue when he said it.

"I hate hospitals," Gregory groaned as he eyed the doctor. "But not you, Doc."

Doctor Ellis turned to Owen. "I understand your position, Owen. I can arrange for a nurse to come in if you must leave. But with it being Christmas, it will be tough. It's nearly impossible to keep the hospital staffed over Christmas."

Gregory's voice was pleading. "Owen. Stay."

Owen remembered the lack of staff just last night. Doctor Ellis was being truthful.

But the thing was that Owen hated being the bad guy. It was a role he'd spent his entire life trying not to pick up. He'd played by society's rules. He was polite even to people he wanted to punch in the mouth at times for their rudeness. He was generous sometimes to a fault. Most of all, he wanted his father to be proud of his accomplishments. He'd graduated top of his class. He'd worked his way through University of Chicago and snagged his masters in less than sixteen months. What he didn't understand was that all he'd done and pushed himself toward, came down to this one moment in a hospital where he looked like the king of all jerks in front of a nurse and his father's doctor. Worse, even to his dad.

"I'll take him home," Owen said as Doctor Ellis slapped him on the back.

"Excellent. I'll get the discharge papers ready immediately."

Gregory grinned from ear to ear.

Owen couldn't help thinking his father looked a bit too happy.

* * * * *

With his hanging bag slung over his shoulder and balancing his suitcase and briefcase in his left hand, Owen opened the front door as Gregory walked up the porch steps with the same spry gait Owen remembered. Gregory didn't use the handrail. He didn't falter. To Owen's mind, he looked to be in perfect health. No one would ever guess he'd just endured a heart attack. Mild or not, his dad had passed out on the floor. Or so Holly substantiated the story.

Beau came bounding down the hall toward them and the force of his one hundred twenty-seven pound body against Owen's leg was enough to knock the hanging bag off Owen's shoulder and onto the floor. "Whoa, Beau!" Owen leaned down to ruffle Beau's ears. "How you been? I guess you missed me."

"We all did," Gregory said hanging his parka on the wall hook. "Let me take your coat."

Owen eased out of his overcoat and eyed his father. "You look pretty good today."

"Thanks."

"It wouldn't surprise me if you faked this heart attack just to get me to come home."

"Trust me, I did not," Gregory said leaning over to pet Beau. "I'll call Holly and thank her for taking care of Beau last night."

"She stayed here? I thought she said she was going home."

"No. She came and got Beau and took him home with her. Then she brought him back this morning."

"So, she has a key to the house? Is that safe? I mean, how long have you known her?"

Gregory halted, put his hand on his hips and said, "You need to lighten up, son. I trust her."

"Dad. Life is different now. You can't be too careful."

Gregory turned. "I'm going to make coffee. You want some?"

"Sure. I'll go put my things away."

"Hopefully, you remember where your room is."

"Dad, let's not do this, okay?"

"Okay! Got it." Gregory shifted his eyes to the Christmas tree. "You didn't say anything about the tree."

Owen looked at the fresh conifer with its natural citrus and pine scent filling the room. It was a fragrance that took him right back to his childhood. Those remembered nostalgic days tumbled across his mind like a slow-motion video. They were the places and people he hadn't dared to visit for fear they would pull him off the bead. Off the grid he was building for his new life away from----"here," he whispered to himself.

Owen looked at his father. "You need to rest. I can't believe it took all morning and then some for the hospital to dismiss you. "

"Paperwork and on computers, no less, that are supposed to speed things up. Ridiculous."

"I believe they were keeping an eye on you. I noticed they didn't remove the EKG and the heart monitor until just before we left. I think they were looking for something."

"Well, they didn't find it, did they?"

"No. Not this time."

"I'm starving. It's nearly dinner time, you must be hungry. Holly left a Shepherd's Pie. You want some?"

"Maybe later. I have work to do." Owen replied pulling his rolling suitcase down the narrow hall.

He walked into his old bedroom and halted. "Not possible."

The walls were still covered with rock concert posters he'd collected in college. There were photographs of all three of his graduations. His mother had lived to see him receive his Masters and that had been a glorious day for the family. Kris had invited all their neighbors, most all the members of the Co-Op, several of his high school friends, all of whom he'd forgotten and left behind when he went away to college. But they'd all been happy for him. His dad had hired a country band to play in the barn and the food his mother had prepared could have fed a battalion. It was her way of showing her love, pride, and happiness. He was their only son. And on that day, he felt he had fulfilled his destiny.

Months later, his mother came down with bronchitis which turned to pneumonia. Gregory found her that morning. He'd called Owen who'd just been promoted in the firm he'd interned with the summer before. He had a studio apartment near Wrigleyville. No furniture to speak of and no food in the 'fridge, but he didn't care. He was making his way in the world. He remembered how he held the phone to his ear that day, stunned and frozen. The impossible had happened.

Owen realized as he put his bags on the twin bed covered in a red and green Christmas plaid spread, that he was still in shock.

"Being here brings it all back. Every digging pain of it."

* * * * *

Gregory smiled broadly as he looked at the homemade banner Holly's kids, Mary and Joe, had made for him. "Get Well, Mr. Michaels. We love you. Mary and Joe." There were dozens of smiley faces on the banner. On the refrigerator were the kids' drawings of Christmas trees and stars.

"Would you look at that, Beau? Those kids could grow up to be artists."

Beau barked his approval and then went over to his water dish, slurped up the remainder of the water and went to lie down on his doggie bed near the back door.

Gregory took the casserole from the refrigerator. It was covered with a glass cover and taped to the top was a handwritten note from Holly. "Glad you are home for Christmas!"

Gregory took out a plate from the cupboard, scooped a large serving of the mashed potatoes topped with cheese and the ground turkey meat and onions below. Holly never cooked with beef. She claimed it was because she loved cows. He thought she had the ulterior motive of trying to lower his cholesterol. He put the plate in the microwave to warm it and poured a large glass of water.

After the microwave beeped, he took the meal and sat at the table. He bowed his head. "Thank you, God, for this food. For my friends Holly and Sam and the kids. And I'm deeply grateful you brought Owen back home."

As hungry as he was, he was surprised how little it took to satisfy him. He glanced at Beau who watched him eagerly. "Guess I'm more tuckered out than I am hungry." He took the plate and placed it on the floor. "Here you go, boy. You finish it off."

Beau jumped up and immediately scarfed down the remaining casserole.

Gregory patted his head, took the plate and went to the sink.

Through the kitchen window above the sink, the wind had picked up considerably as night had fallen. Gregory watched as the trees swayed and then bent with the strong winds. Suddenly, lightning cracked across the sky. Thunder boomed.

"That's strange. I have never seen lightning this time of year." He shuffled across the floor. "C'mon, Beau. Let's hit the hay."

Gregory put on his flannel pajamas, brushed his teeth and washed his hands and face as Beau jumped up on the bed and settled into his usual position at the foot of the bed on stormy nights. Outside the window, the storm continued to howl as Gregory got into bed and covered up.

"Don't worry, boy. You're always safe with me."

Owen had finally found the Wi-fi connection and had his laptop up and running. He had just finished changing into jeans and an old sweatshirt, when his cell phone rang.

"Julia. You got my text, huh?"

"I did. I'm not happy about it, though."

"Even if I could come back tonight the weather is bad here." Owen went to the window and watched as jagged lightning bolts lit the sky.

"It is clear and lovely here. But listen, you can stay there till Christmas Eve. But you must be back here for the Gala and my parents' brunch."

"I'll do my best. Let's play it by ear."

"You know I hate it when you say that," she complained. "I need things…."

"Scheduled. Neat and tidy. I know."

As Owen watched the sky, an enormous lightning bolt shot across the top of the big hill where Gregory had cut down the Christmas tree. The bolt appeared to linger for a long moment, lighting the terrain and sky around it.

"What the---? That was bad! I hope we don't lose power."

"What's going on?" Julia asked.

"This storm. It's too late for lightning storms. And there's been no rain. Just wind and lightning. Plus, I haven't heard that much thunder. It's like the lightning strikes are miles and miles from here…but…"

"Oh, Owen. Is this part of your astronomy fascination?"

"It's curious."

* * * * *

The powerful lightning storm rattled the window in Gregory's room, waking both him and Beau. Beau growled.

Gregory sat up, petted Beau's head to calm him and went to the window. At the top of the hill was a glowing light that appeared to grow brighter, then pulse from silver white to a golden glow. He put on his glasses.

"What in the world is going on?"

Gregory went to his chair, picked up his robe, stuck his feet in his slippers and then went to the living room and grabbed his parka. With Beau following him, they went to the kitchen and exited the house through the back kitchen door. Gregory was careful to hold onto the back porch railing as he descended the steps. There was a light snow on the ground, but neither he nor Beau minded.

"See that gold light? It's still there, Beau." Gregory crossed the yard and began climbing the hill. It had been months since he'd walked this hill. He'd taken to driving the tractor up and down. But he didn't mind the frosty air, or the difficulty he had breathing. The golden glow beckoned him as if he were in a trance.

Owen was still on the phone with Julia. "I think the lightning set a tree on fire out there."

"Oh my God! Is it close to the house? Are you in danger?"

"No, it's a long way off, but the wind is strong…." Owen put his face closer to the window. "The wind stopped. I mean completely stopped. And…. wait a minute."

Seeing two figures, a man, and a dog, walking up the hill, Owen sucked in a breath. "Dad? Oh holy…Julia, I gotta go."

"Owen?"

Without another word to Julia, Owen ended the call and tossed his cell phone on the bed. He stuck his feet in his running shoes and bolted out of the room, down the hall and to the kitchen.

"Dad!" Owen shouted as he shot down the back porch and across the yard. "Dad! What the hell are you doing?"

Gregory made it to the top of the hill as Owen ran after him shouting. But Gregory was compelled to uncover the mystery of the still glowing white light.

"Dad! Are you crazy? Dad!"

Gregory moved to the white light that was now dimming. All he saw was a pile of white feathers as if someone had shot down a large swan. "Yep, must be a bird all right. There is a wing."

Beau sniffed the ground around the area, not satisfied that he could identify any scent. Yet.

Gregory reached down to inspect the wing. "Maybe it's still alive and we can take this swan to the vet." When he shook the feathers, the wing disappeared and he felt a bare shoulder.

"What in the…."

Beau barked.

A gust of wind blew and scattered the white feathers down the hill in a series of tiny whirlwinds. On the ground was a young, beautiful woman with very long blonde hair. She was dressed in a gossamer thin white gown, tied at the shoulders with gold clips fashioned like wings. She was barefoot and the only cover she had was her long hair. Slowly she opened her eyes and looked at Gregory. She shivered. Then shivered again.

"Shalom," Angel said as she realized this was Gregory whom she'd come to earth to see.

"Huh?"

"Bonjour?" Angel said in French. Already this earth was more difficult than she'd expected. Gone was the eternal daylight in heaven. This body she had acquired was heavy, dense, and extremely uncomfortable when she'd only known the warm compassionate atmosphere of her home. Added to all that, Angel B-2222 had warned her that humans used language to communicate rather than telepathy. She remembered that on earth there were a myriad of languages. She had to find the correct one or her mission would end in disaster.

Gregory smiled at her. "Hello."

"Ah! English. Hello." She returned his smile knowing that she had a chance at being successful with her mission.

"Are you all right?" Gregory asked.

Angel tried to answer, but her body continued to shake and her teeth chattered.

"You're cold," Gregory stated.

"C…C…cold?"

Angel wrapped her arms about her middle, but it did little to stop the shivering.

"Your lips are turning blue," Gregory observed.

Angel remembered the download about the human body. She touched her lips and felt her mouth.

"Lips. The human communication device."

"What?" Gregory shook his head and laughed.

She looked at him. "You're not telepathic."

"I wish."

"Wishing is a start," she agreed.

Owen was out of breath when he reached the top of the hill. The climb was enough to give anyone a heart attack, he thought, but his father was breathing normally. Too concerned with his father's health, he didn't notice that his father was holding the hand of a woman. A young woman who was wearing a sheer nightgown and no shoes on a blustery, freezing night.

"Dad. Who is this?"

Angel's face broke into a smile of recognition. "I…. saw you…."

"Yeah? Where was that?"

Angel couldn't answer due to the chattering of her teeth. Her back had tensed from the cold she was in what she been told was called pain. She did not like pain. It was awful and she wanted it stopped.

Gregory took off his parka and put it on Angel. "You are freezing. Here put this on." He had to help her put her arms in the parka.

"What's your name?" Owen asked bluntly.

"Name?"

"Yes." Owen demanded.

Gregory scowled at Owen. "Son…"

"Please, Dad. We need to know who she is."

"An….gel…uh…"

Gregory beamed. "Angela. Beautiful name. Now are you satisfied, Owen? We need to get her to the house and warm her up before we have to call 911 again!" Gregory put his arm around Angela to help her stand.

"Dad, we need to know who she is and where she's from."

"We can ask questions later. She'll catch pneumonia out here."

His father's words bit into Owen like a knife. Pneumonia had killed his mother. Of course, his father would be concerned. "Okay. Right. You're right."

"What's pneumonia?" Angel asked.

"You never heard of pneumonia?"

"No. And can I catch it with my hands? Or do I need an implement to catch it? Like a fishnet? I saw those once when I was observing the Sea of Galilee. But that was a long time ago in earth years."

"Earth years," Owen mused. "Anyway, pneumonia is a serious medical condition that can lead to death if you don't take care of yourself."

"What's death?" She asked as she stumbled and nearly brought Gregory down with her.

Owen rolled his eyes. "Dad, I'll help her down. You aren't all that steady on your feet yet, either.

"Good idea, son."

Owen put his arm around Angel's shoulder. "Can you walk?"

"Walk? I usually fly."

"Sorry. No planes around here."

Gregory took one of Angel's arms. "For heaven's sake, Owen. Just help her."

With both men taking one of Angel's arms, they helped her down the snowy hill to the house. Owen understood his father had expended far too much energy that evening. He was not about to let a strange talking woman disrupt Gregory's recovery.

When they entered the kitchen, Owen said, "Dad, you've had enough for one day. I'll make her some cocoa and you go back to bed."

Gregory nodded. "You're right. I'm tuckered."

Owen searched his father's face. "You okay? Really."

"I will be, son. A good night's sleep…sounds good." Gregory pulled up a white bentwood chair with a Christmas plaid seat cushion. "This was my wife's chair. It's comfy. You sit here. I'll see you both in the morning."

"Good night, Dad." Owen said.

"Schlaf gut," Angel said looking at Owen's curious expression. "Sleep well, Gregory."

Owen had just opened the refrigerator door to withdraw the milk when he heard Angela's reply to his father's parting words. He halted mid- motion as the hairs on the back of his neck rose. There was much to consider about this stranger in their house.

She appeared out of nowhere. Barely dressed in freezing cold weather, which first led him to believe she was attempting suicide by hypothermia. She spoke in riddles. She claimed not to know the simplest terms like death. She was breathtakingly beautiful which normally would draw him to her, but rather he wanted to keep her at arm's length. A few hundred miles would be preferable.

In his estimation she was a nut case.

But there was something about her----- He couldn't put his finger on it and that bugged him.

He took out sugar, cocoa and stirred them into the milk on the stove and cooked the mixture on medium. While the cocoa warmed, he went to the kitchen coat rack and took a wool cardigan sweater off the rack and gave it to Angela. "Put this on. It will be long on you and keep you very warm."

"Danke."

Angela took off the parka and when she did, she twisted in the chair, touched her shoulders, and realized that her wings were gone. She'd been so cold from the weather that she hadn't noticed they were missing. It was hard enough making these legs carry her down the hard surface of the earth, not to mention the struggle to activate her now human brain functions just to process thoughts and follow what humans referred to as reasoning.

Navigating earth was already proving to be more than a challenge. This was a gauntlet. She could only pray she didn't turn out to be the ultimate angelic fool of all eternity. Truly, her curiosity rode a second chariot to her naivete.

Owen put marshmallows in two mugs and poured the hot cocoa over them. He placed a mug in front of her and sat in the chair opposite her. "It's hot. Blow on it."

She looked at him quizzically.

"Like this." He blew on the surface of the cocoa and took a sip. It was as good as his mother used to make.

Angela followed his movements, but the cocoa dribbled down her mouth and chin. She choked.

"You okay?" Owen asked.

"It's not cold…like outside."

"No, it's hot. You drink your cocoa cold?"

"I don't drink cocoa."

"You're kidding. This is your first time?"

"Yes. First time---for everything."

She lifted the mug and drank again. Then another and then she downed almost the entire mug full.

Her face burst into glowing happiness.

"I like this cocoa very much."

"Good. Because I made a large batch. We have a lot to talk about."

"About?"

Owen wrapped his hands around his cocoa mug. "That's a beautiful gown you're wearing. You were at a party?"

"Party?"

"And a fancy one, I'm guessing. Those gold wing clips on your shoulders. They look like real gold."

"We all wear gold."

"We?"

"The other ang…Uh, er, people do," she smiled sheepishly.

"And where is your home?"

"Heaven is home."

"Heaven?"

"It's your home, too. You're real home," she replied confidently.

He rose to get more cocoa. He poured another mug for both and then turned on the faucet to wash out the pan. "I sure hope not for a long time."

"Oh, I understand that about humans."

Owen turned off the faucet. "I missed that. So, what brought you here?"

She beamed. "Oh, I rode the lightning bolt."

Owen burst into laughter. "You are too much. Seriously. Did you have a car accident? How is that you were on our hillside?"

She paused for a moment as she realized that he was trying to trick her with his words. She'd been naive to come here. But she had faith. She had to keep believing. "I wanted to help."

"Ah! Another of my father's community friends. So, you heard about his heart attack?"

"No."

Owen inhaled deeply. This woman was screwy enough to make anyone lose their mind. She certainly made him lose his train of thought. "Look, we need to get down to it. The truth. Where you are from and how you got here. But first, since none of us has ever met before, I want to know how you know my dad's name.

* * * * *

Six

Angela took the last slug of the delicious cocoa. She didn't know how to describe it, but it warmed her body from the mouth all the way to her middle. It was like swallowing love. It was rich and sweet. Velvety and gave her a jolt of elation. It was much like the energy blast she received when one of the other angels admired her work. Or when the news came to her that an artist on one of the planets in Andromeda had thanked her for her assistance. Andromedins were discerning and precise. She had to work hard for them.

"So?" Owen pushed. "How did you know his name? Did you investigate him and this farm before showing up here? Believe me there's no fortune on a dairy farm. There's no money. And there's no way you can worm your way into being named in his Will. I handle all his estate. The inheritance is secure."

"I don't want money." She put her cup down.

"What do you want?"

"More cocoa," she beamed.

Owen shook his finger at her. "Oh, no you don't. Not till you tell me about knowing his name."

She had put Gregory's parka on the back of the chair in which she was sitting. Now that she was wearing the long sweater, she was much warmer. She stroked her hand over the long sleeve. "This is warm and soft like angel feathers."

"Interesting analogy."

Instantly, she knew he'd tricked her. She had not responded correctly. She was probably making a lot of mistakes with this human man. She wasn't used to being interrogated nor to surmising situations incorrectly. Truth was truth. But Owen didn't want or seek the truth. He wanted answers that fit his narrow paradigm. "It feels like a cloud." She smiled at him knowing that he responded well to smiles.

"Yes it is. It's cashmere. I gave it to dad last Christmas."

"It's good you care for him."

He looked at her oddly. There was something about her and her words that made him cross-reference his own thoughts. Why would she say that? He didn't know her and she didn't know anything about them.

She turned slightly, lifted the sleeve of the parka and pointed to an embroidered name in gold on the dark blue parka. "His name.... is here. Gregory Michaels."

Owen leaned back in his chair. "I had that monogrammed on the parka. It was a special they were running," he remembered. "You're observant. I gotta give you that."

"That's been said about me."

"I'll bite. Who said that?"

"Oh, an angel told me." She finished her second mug of cocoa.

"I stick with tangible information. The facts. Such as the fact that my dad is going to be fine."

"Are you so very sure?"

"Doctor said so."

"A physician ---of the body."

Owen squirmed in his chair. Why did her words continue to set him on edge? He felt that kind of hesitation where time stood still and the air was suffused with anticipation waiting for the wrecking ball to be released. "Yes," he said hesitantly.

"But his heart is broken."

Owen gathered his calm. "And with rest, he'll be good as new."

"It's love he needs."

Owen rose to his feet as if the hot seat she'd put him on would explode. "It's getting late. I suppose your family will be looking for you." He took the mugs, went to the sink and began washing them.

"No," she replied simply.

"I can drive you home."

"Oh, I don't think so. I'll stay here," she looked back at him with wide eyes.

"Here? Tonight?" Owen hadn't once thought this bizarre night would come to this. A strange woman in the house. One who was clearly either a throwback to a 1960's flower child or she was off her meds.

"That would be suitable. And best."

Owen looked at the clock and was surprised to see it was well after midnight. "I had no idea it was so late. I suppose you could take my room and I can sleep on the daybed in my mom's old sewing room."

"Sleep. Yes. Dreamtime."

"Cute." He dried his hands on a towel. "Okay. Follow me. I'll show you where everything is. But I'll need my pillow."

"Pillow?"

"It's special. I've had it since I was in high school."

"A sentiment."

"You could say that."

Angela followed Owen out of the kitchen and down the hall to Owen's bedroom. She liked the large window that looked out onto the moonlit rolling back yard and up the hill with the trees and evergreens. The night sky was clear and though she couldn't see other galaxies, she thought the stars were very pretty from earth.

She sat down on the bed.

"This is my bed," he said pushing down on the mattress. "I hope it's not too firm for you."

"I like it."

He went to the closet and pulled out a couple blankets. "Here's an extra blanket for you," he said reaching behind her. He moved very close to her neck, and when he did, he was overwhelmed by the scent of roses. It reminded him again of his mother.

"You smell like roses," he said softly moving slowly backward.

"We all do. I love roses."

"Me, too."

He felt stupefied as if he'd been drugged. He rubbed his eyes to clear the haze from his vision wondering what was wrong. He knew it was late. He needed sleep. That's all it was.

As Owen walked over to the door, he stumbled over his briefcase. "Ouch!"

"What is it?"

"I stubbed my toe. It hurts."

"Yes. Pain. I understand."

He looked at Angela sitting on the bed, staring at him. The lamp on the bedside table glowed behind her, but there was another glow that looked like pearlescent light shimmering off a waterfall. It clung to her cascading hair and created an aura around her. Her blue eyes met his and when they did, he was riveted to the spot. He couldn't move. Didn't want to move. He didn't believe in hypnosis, spells, or magic traps. Something was happening to him. But what?

His tongue was tied but somehow, he managed to say, "Goodnight, then."

"Sleep with the angels," she smiled.

Owen gaped. "That's what my mother always said to me every night of her life."

"I'm sure she still does. You just don't hear her."

The cobwebs in Owen's brain thickened and all thoughts drained from him as he turned and went to the sewing room. He wrapped the blanket around him, still wondering why he was experiencing so many strange sensations. It was confusing and thought provoking down unfamiliar paths. His mind was overloaded.

He laid down on the sofa bed and was instantly asleep.

* * * * *

The door to Owen's bedroom had not closed all the way and through the opening, Beau marched into the room. He took one look at Angela and jumped up on the bed and placed his head in her lap. She soothed his head.

"Hello, Beau," she said telepathically.

Beau didn't move, but Angela heard his thoughts clearly. "I've always wanted my own Angel."

"You have me, now."

"Good. These humans need help," Beau offered.

"I'm seeing that. I hope I arrived in time."

"I hope so," Beau added.

"You've been with them for a long time. Are they as difficult as they appear?"

"Worse."

Angela's shoulders slumped. "Not good."

* * * * *

Seven

Angela welcomed the first golden ray of dawn light with relief that the long hours of darkness were over and she could be about the Creator's work. She had rested only momentarily, since she didn't need sleep like humans did. Her night hours were spent conferring with other angels still on The Other Side about strategies and methodologies regarding human psychology and how to proceed regarding her mission.

Initially, she'd had so much compassion for Owen. But meeting the man in this environment was already proving to be more challenging than she had thought. He was opinionated, a bit egotistical and controlling. He was the kind of human who believed they could control destiny. She shook her head. "Let go and let God."

The rules of the universe were so simple. Humans didn't like simple. They wanted to complicate everything.

She rose from the bed, still wearing her gown and the sweater. She'd noticed that there were many clothes behind the doors in a cubicle that Owen referred to as a closet. She noticed that both Owen and Gregory wore a thick textured covering on their legs to keep warm in the unfriendly atmosphere outside the confines of the warm house. She found a pair of dark blue pants hanging from a rack. When she put them on, they fell off her body. She took the gold clips from her gown and used them to hold the waist together. The pants slid down to her hips. She grabbed a thick roll of the fabric and held onto it. Then she rolled up the bottom of the leg to her ankles. She found a pair of foot coverings and put her feet in them. They were far too big and fell off her feet.

Frowning, about the foot wear issue, she selected a black chest covering that was similar to the sweater Owen had provided for her, but this covering had a unit that fit over her head. She wore this covering over the soft cashmere sweater.

She picked up the big shoes, still holding the pants up at the waist, she walked out to the kitchen with Beau following behind her. She filled his bowl with water and put it on the floor. "What else do you eat?" She asked the dog.

"Anything I can beg from off the table. Since there's no breakfast yet, there's some awful dog food in that big bag in the pantry closet. I'll show you." Beau padded over to the pantry and hit the door with his paw. "In here."

Angela went into the pantry and found the big blue bag. She dipped Beau's food bowl into the bag and set it on the floor next to his water. He took a few bites. "I'd rather have pancakes and bacon."

"I don't know what they are but I'll tell Gregory."

"He makes good pancakes. And he shares. It is good."

Angela rummaged in the pantry and withdrew a paper bag, wire, and a pair of sheers. She put the too large shoes on and tromped to the back door.

Beau looked up from his water. "Where are you going?"

"Owen's mother downloaded a lot of information for me last night. Besides language lessons, and information about Owen and Gregory, she said she doesn't like the wreath on the front door. She told me about a holly bush nearby and cedar sprigs and how to make the wreath. You want to come?"

"I do."

As she shut the kitchen door behind her, she said, "Being an angel on earth is not so bad when I get so much spiritual help. Too bad humans do not ask for it."

"Too bad."

* * * * *

Angela sat on the kitchen floor with the grocery store wreath from the front door in her lap as she twisted and tied pieces of holly, red berries and the elegant draping cedar sprigs whose shape reminded her of angel feathers.

She'd found it impossible to work in Owen's too large clothes that kept falling off. She changed back into her white gown and cashmere sweater.

The night before while Kris was instructing her how to affix the holly to the wreath and the proper placement of the cedar springs, Angela had formed a mental picture in her head of how the wreath should look. When Gregory walked into the kitchen in slippers and pajamas, the wreath was finished.

"Good morning," he said. "And my—Isn't that beautiful. Just like Kris used to make."

Angela smiled and looked from the wreath back to Gregory. "It is, isn't it?"

Dressed in suit and tie, Owen walked from the hall to the kitchen, stared at Angela and said, "Good morning."

"A blessed day to you."

Gregory pointed to the holly. "Where did those greens come from?"

Angela placed another piece of holly. "Oh, I asked the trees outside if I could have them."

Owen slapped his forehead. "You 'asked' the trees?"

"Um. And the holly bush as well."

Owen's head fell backward on his neck. "God."

Gregory touched Angela's bare shoulder. "You'll be dead from a chill before Sunday. Wait here."

Owen spun around as Gregory left the room. "Dad? What are you doing?"

"Back in a minute, son."

Owen stepped over the mess of spruce sprigs that smelled all at once too nostalgic and too enchanting, taking him back to decades past when his mother sat on the floor exactly like Angela, even barefoot, now that he thought about it. And the wreath was identical to the ones his mother made.

He went to the coffee pot, filled it with water and measured out the coffee, pretending he did NOT feel goosebumps on his arms and neck. Pretending he was NOT affected by the scene on the floor. It was just an ordinary perfect stranger, as beautiful as a goddess, forming a wreath with an artistry that he would have sworn only his mother could create. He was living a dream. Maybe this wasn't real at all and he was experiencing a hologram or new time line. After all, quantum physics had proven it possible.

The rustling and falling items from the hall closet brought Owen's attention back to the present. "Dad? What on earth are you doing?"

Gregory's happy smile was concealed by the mound of clothes he carried. He'd brought women's slacks, blouses, pajamas, sweaters, and a pair of hiking boots dangling from his hand.

"Dad, what are you doing?" Owen didn't like his father's gesture one bit. Gregory was becoming attached to Angela far too quickly. Perhaps it was loneliness. Maybe his father had a crush on the gorgeous woman. It could happen. Owen was keenly aware of the cruelty that occurred when a young and beautiful woman sought out an elderly man. Gold diggers. Fortune hunters. It went both ways. And the scenario was the same. Heartbreak for the trusting elder.

Owen didn't get Angela's game.

She was kind and polite and now helpful. But she was obviously weaving her way into their home and life. She had an agenda.

One of the most valuable roles an estate planner played was that of bad cop. He was the private detective that weeded out the greedy grandkids. The relatives that would cheat an angel to take what they falsely believed to be theirs from a family estate.

Iron clad documents were security. Owen was glad he had protected his father that way.

So, he'd already warned Angela there was no money to be had here at the Michaels farm.

What could possibly be her agenda?

Maybe she was truly homeless and penniless. Maybe she needed the warm clothes and a bed. Maybe she needed food. Nah, he thought. Not the food. She doesn't know what to do with it.

Gregory said to Angela, "These belonged to Owen's mother, Kris. They're outdated. But they'll keep you warm."

"You are very kind."

"Dad. I'm sure Angela has plenty of clothes at her own home."

"They're all like this," she replied, standing up and gesturing to the gorgeous gown.

"So, you live in the South?" Owen probed.

Frowning at Owen, Gregory handed the clothes to Angela. "Take them to your room and try them on."

Gregory watched as Angela left the room with Beau fast on her heels. He scratched his head. "That's odd."

Owen poured his coffee into a mug. "Everything about Angela is odd. To what specifically are you referring?"

"Beau. He's never trusted anyone. Me. You. Holly and the kids. That's it. But he took to Angela without a beat."

Owen looked up from his coffee. "Oh?" His eyes went to the hallway. "Mysteries. I've never liked mysteries."

Gregory picked up the wreath and inspected it. "Then here's another one. This wreath looks exactly like the ones your mother made. And the spool of wire is untouched. She tied the branches together inside the wreath. Maybe she's a florist."

"Whatever she is, I intend to find out and fast."

"What are you saying?"

"Dad. She appears out of nowhere. She told me she rode a lightning bolt to earth. She didn't even know how to drink cocoa much less what it was. Every kid has cocoa at least once."

"Not every. But what's your point?"

Owen placed his mug on the counter and leveled serious eyes on his father. "I think she's a runaway from that sanitarium."

A frustrated breath escaped Gregory's lips. "It's a dementia and Alzheimer's assisted living facility."

"It used to be a sanitarium."

"They sold out to this new group."

"Which is now called?" Owen pushed his intractable father.

"Heavenly Acres."

Owen slapped his thigh. "Ha! Heavenly Acres. Exactly. When I asked her where she was from she said, 'Heaven.'"

"That's a figure of speech," Gregory countered.

"Yeah? For whom? Mentally impaired patients?" Owen struck back.

Gregory's hand flew to his chest. Owen bolted toward him and eased him into a chair.

"Crap. You okay, Dad?"

"A---twinge."

"See? Angela's brought on anxiety already. I'm taking her back there this morning."

"No, son. It's okay. I'm okay."

"Face it, Dad. You're getting attached to her. She's a stranger. A strange stranger. I think she reminds you of mom."

Gregory waved his hand dismissively. "Never. I see your mom everyday."

"You what?"

A loud knock on the door interrupted their conversation. Owen went to the window and lifted the curtain. Standing on the porch was Holly and next to her was a tall, handsome, and very fit man wearing boots, a plaid wool work jacket and work gloves.

"Who is it?" Gregory asked.

"It's Holly and think this must be Sam, her husband."

"Well, let them in out of the cold, for heaven's sake."

Owen opened the door and greeted them politely. He noticed they were carrying covered dishes with food that all smelled of cinnamon, maple syrup and bacon. Owen's mouth watered.

"Holly. Nice to see you. And," he said turning to Sam, "You must be Sam. I'm Owen."

From behind Holly and Sam peaked a little boy and girl.

"Owen," Holly began. "These are our children. This is Joey. He's eight."

Joey who slipped off his knit cap revealing a military buzz haircut, then stepped forward, stuck out his hand for Owen to shake. "Hello, Mr. Michaels. You can call me Joe. I help my dad a lot around the farm. Isn't that right, Mr. Michaels?" Joe looked at Gregory.

"Sure do."

There's nothing shy about this kid, Owen thought as he shook the boy's hand.

"And this is Mary."

The slender, blonde girl with a long thick braid falling down the back of her pink parka and wearing jeans and pink snow boots, smiled winningly at Owen. "I'm seven. I'm in the first grade and first in my class in spelling and I can already read at third grade level."

"Wow!" Owen bit back a smile. "That's amazing."

"I'm good at math, too. I help Mr. Michaels with the bills and receipts," Mary added quickly.

Gregory laughed. "I don't see the numbers as well as I used to. She's a big help."

"I'll bet."

Holly put the casserole dishes on the counter. "We wanted to see how Greg was doing today. I brought a French toast casserole the kids like."

"Yeah," Joe said. "It has a lot of bacon and syrup."

"And some breakfast burritos and scones. Depending on what everyone felt like."

"Thank you," Owen said. "It looks like a lot of work. I could go down to Murphy's and bring back something."

"Absolutely not!" Holly protested. "That woman cooks with dirty grease. I do not like Greg eating that food any more than necessary."

"Now, Holly," Gregory huffed up his chest. "She's not the only reason for my high cholesterol."

"Well, it's not from my cooking, that you can bet on."

Sam put his arm on Holly's shoulder. "The kids and I better get to work."

"Work?" Owen asked looking at Mary. "What do you do besides be a CPA?"

"I don't know what that is, but I help with the calves," she replied proudly.

Joe stuck his knit cap back on. "And I drive the tractor to clean up the manure from the cow barn when my dad marches the cows to the milking parlor."

Surprised, Owen's eyes widened. "You drive the tractor? Aren't you a little…"

"I'm almost nine," Joe interrupted.

Sam laughed. "He wanted to start when he was seven."

"Yeah, but I couldn't reach the pedals."

Sam continued. "And Mary here, she also helps her mother in the kitchen."

Mary jumped in. "I loooove making cookies. Especially the ones for the Christmas Cookie Exchange at the Town Center."

Owen glanced at his father. "They still have that?"

"Sure do."

Owen shook his head and looked out the window. Once again, he was taken back. "My mother started that Exchange. She loved this town a lot. She loved this community."

Holly's voice was soft when she replied, "That's what your dad said."

"I remember the sugar cookies she made. So, buttery. I frosted them. Too many sprinkles, though."

Giggling, Mary cooed, "I love sprinkles."

Angela stood in the doorway to the kitchen with Beau at her side. She was wearing blue jeans rolled up at the ankles, hiking boots and a pink blouse with a frilly collar that encircled her throat. She had brushed out her hair into a voluminous mane that caught the morning sun through the window and created a radiant glow around her. Everyone in the room stopped talking and stared.

She's a vision...a mirage that could evaporate any second. He was enthralled, when he didn't want to be. Again, his brain slipped into a stupor.

"Owen," Holly nudged. "Who's this?"

"Uh. Sorry. This is Angela. She, er, arrived last night."

Holly stepped past Own and Gregory. She extended her hand to Angela. "Hello, Angela. I'm Holly---we're neighbors."

"You're family," Gregory corrected.

Angela looked down at Holly's hand, smiled up at her and then embraced Holly with a warm hug. "You are bright. Love."

"Why, thank you, Angela." She turned. "This is my husband, Sam. And my children---

"Mary and Joseph," Angela finished.

"Why, yes."

Owen scrunched his eyes as he peered at Angela. "Did I tell you their names? I did, right?"

Angela only smiled at him. Then looked back at Holly, telepathically suggesting Holly look at the wreath.

"What a beautiful wreath." Holly gushed as she picked it up.

"It's for the front door."

"A Christmas wreath." Owen's eyes were fastened on Angela. He didn't know why, but she grew more beautiful with every graceful movement. He could see why his father was infatuated. If he didn't already have Julia, he'd be into Angela. Too easily.

"The Egyptians popularized them," Angela said wondering if her knowledge of ancient earth civilizations was of any interest to them. For the first time she was aware that Owen was looking at her for an inordinate amount of time. The others in the room darted their eyes from one another. The children glanced at their parents. They shuffled their feet.

They were uncomfortable.

"And they never went out of style," Gregory chuckled breaking the silence.

Sam clapped his hands. "Well, kids. Holly. We better get to work. Those cows can't wait."

Gregory started to rise. "I should help."

"NO!" the shout came from every mouth. Even Angela.

Gregory sat back down. "Guess not, huh?"

"Dad, you need to rest."

Gregory's disappointment was evident to everyone. He had always been a working man, never complaining about the on-coming of the years, but this heart attack had changed everything for him. His polarity had shifted and now he was face to face with the end of him.

Angela went to him, put her arm around him. "I'll help you to your room. Rest is the quickest path to healing."

As he rose, he patted her hand. "My wife used to say that all the time."

Owen's head snapped up. "She did?" His eyes met Angela's. He couldn't help wondering how she knew these little tell all's about his mother. They should all add up. *But to what end?*

"Thank you, Angela," Gregory said as she led him out of the kitchen.

* * * * *

Angela helped Gregory to his room. He was tired but still steady on his feet. Beau followed them down the hall.

"Your wife was a wise woman," Angela said.

"She's been gone many years," he replied.

"She's not gone. She's right here with you."

They stopped at the doorway.

"Thank you for saying that, Angela. I do believe she never left me. I'll be all right now."

Angela waited till Gregory sat down on the edge of the bed. Beau followed him into the room. She looked at Beau. "Will you take over now for me?"

"Sure, Angel 7777."

Startled, Angel asked, "Who told you my name?"

Beau shook his head and snorted. "I promised not to tell."

"Oh, so that's how it will be," she laughed.

"Yes. And you have a job to do," Beau said telepathically.

"You know about that, too?"

"Yes. I'm at your service. It's why they let me hear your thoughts and mine yours."

Knowing Beau would take good care of his master, Angela went back to the kitchen.

They were all awaiting her report.

"He'll rest now."

Sam put his arm around Holly's shoulder. "Good. Well, come on, kids. We have work to do."

Mary looked up at Holly. "But Mom, when are we going to make the cookies?"

"Uh, tomorrow."

"Aw, mom," Mary protested as Holly smiled back to Owen and Angela and waved.

When they left Owen didn't waste a minute moving on his agenda for the day. "Since you don't have a coat, I'll give you a parka."

"Why?"

"It's cold outside. I'm taking you somewhere." He went to the hall hooks and took a parka down and held it up for her. She stared at him as if she didn't know what to do. "Turn around."

Angela turned around. He took her arm and put it in one sleeve. She grabbed the parka and put her arm in the other sleeve.

"I can do this," she replied sweetly. "I want to learn how to make cookies. What are they?"

Owen struggled into his own coat, suddenly perplexed again at her odd questions. "You don't know what cookies are? Or are you diabetic?"

"I don't know what diabetic is, but the cookies appear to make children happy."

"It's the sugar."

"Sugar. Hmm."

Owen put his hand on the small of Angela's back to steer her out of the kitchen. This was something he'd only done with Julia. Not even Amanda, his former girlfriend, because he'd known she wasn't the "right" one for him. This was a boyfriend-girlfriend gesture. It was a significator of caring and protection to one's mate. But Angela was none of those things, yet his hand felt more comfortable, more at home, more caring on Angela's back than it did on Julia's.

And that was another problem.

He admitted it. Angela magnetized him. There it was. He'd known her less than a day and she'd filled his consciousness with her ---essence. He knew he couldn't be in love with her. He didn't know her. Besides, he was in love with Julia. Hadn't he just bought Julia expensive diamond earrings.

But they were not a diamond ring.

Owen hated it the way his sub-conscious could cut to the chase about some things. Personal things. Maybe he did possess intuition like his mother had. He'd never tested it because he didn't believe in it. If things didn't add up logically, that meant they were non-sensical. That meant the Angela was mentally deficient, needed professional help and he needed to be away from her.

Out of sight. Out of mind.

She was smiling at him again as if she knew more than he did. She drove him crazy.

"I'll help the children when I come back.

"Uh, that won't be happening."

"I think it will."

* * * * *

Eight

Angela watched while Owen walked in front of the automobile after settling her in her seat. *So,* she thought. *This is the conveyance they use to move from one location to another. I'd much rather fly. How I miss my wings.* She looked out the window and up to the sky. *It would have been prudent on your part to allow me to hear human thoughts.*

It was more than a struggle to understand humans. It was impossible. And she'd always believed that anything was possible with God. Well, this wasn't. And of all the people, Owen was the most difficult. Because she was able to psychically "body scan" and "soul scan" humans, she knew he had built an energetic dark wall around his heart. *That* she could see with her heart. She didn't need telepathy to figure that one out. He was a study in personality and soul. Indeed, it was her curiosity that brought her to earth and it was her greatest lesson to be given the most difficult of souls to break open.

Fortunately, she wasn't a warrior angel or an archangel who had to deal with dark entities, fallen angels and beasts. They had their assignments and she had hers.

However, she would be very curious to see if even one, just one of the archangels would be able to show Owen Michaels what his true lesson was. The rules of the Universe were cut and dried. She could not interfere when or where she was not invited.

It had been Gregory's prayer that brought her to earth.

Owen probably didn't realize that he'd prayed for her intervention as well.

Sort of.

She deduced that even the Celestial Council of Light of Twenty-Four stretched the rules a smidge on that one.

Now that she was here, there was no doubt, no question she was needed.

"I'm committed," she reiterated to the heavens. "I will not step away."

Owen climbed into his BMW and buckled his seat belt. He stared at her.

"Well?"

"What?"

"Buckle up."

She stared back blankly.

"Your seat belt."

She leaned forward and looked through the windshield at the sky.

"What---are you doing now?" Frustration filtered through his every word.

"Looking for Orion's belt."

"Oh, for Pete's sake---" He reached over, grabbed the seat belt, and buckled it for her. His face skimmed her cheek. He felt a zing of electricity go straight to his heart. He blinked. His breath caught in his esophagus. If he'd dropped into a time-warp, he wouldn't have been shocked.

"The restraint."

Her breath skittered across his cheek like the brush of a butterfly wing. He was in it again. Mesmerized. He struggled not to let himself fall into the depths of her sky-blue eyes. But he failed.

"Angela."

She blinked and the moment passed.

"Yes, I meant the restraint," he said not knowing how he could possibly form any words.

"My mistake," she whispered. "For always looking up."

"Right. Right."

He settled back in his seat. Pressed the start button and backed the car around. He drove carefully down the farmhouse drive. Very. Very carefully.

Through the night, two or more inches of snow had fallen, lacing the skeletons of the maple and oak trees along the roadside. The evergreens looked like grand court ladies in white gowns that glittered in the morning sunlight. The countryside was magical winter at its best.

"It is so cold as to cause pain, but the beauty brings warmth to my heart," she said.

"Poetic," he mused as he turned on the radio. The radio announcers voice was like glass breaking to Angela.

"Twelve dead in a mass gun slaying. The shooter turned the gun on himself at the end of the killing spree."

The power and force of the dark news caused Angela to place her hand on her heart, pray for the souls coming into heaven and to cry for the humans on earth who would miss them. The emotions she felt were vicious and unsettling. She didn't know how humans could spend one minute; one day in such a dark vibration.

She pointed her finger at the radio. The news reporter was cut off and in his place was the peaceful, beautiful music of Yo-Yo Ma.

"Almost like home," she exhaled and let her head fall back on the headrest.

Owen fumbled with the radio controls on his steering wheel.

"I must have hit something."

"But not the right note," she said.

Owen shot her a quizzical glance just as his GPS announced that he'd arrived at his destination. The Heavenly

Acres Residential Community sign was half obliterated with the snow cover from the night before.

He turned into the white fence-lined, plowed driveway and drove up to a well-constructed brick building with two story high Grecian pillars on the front veranda. There was an Evergreen tree on the front lawn filled with suet shaped bells covered with birdseed that attracted a half dozen cardinals. Garlands draped the front doors and cheery Christmas wreaths hung on all the first-floor windows. On the far left of the building was a lighted manger, and a Christmas sleigh that was filled with shiny wrapped boxes.

"This is beautiful," Angela chimed.

"Let's go in," Owen suggested unbuckling Angela's seat belt.

The smell of pine and cinnamon from a decorated live Christmas tree in the lobby caused Angela to pause and sniff the air. Dozens of poinsettias decorated every table top and the sofa tables behind large comfortable looking sofas in the large carpeted reception area. From a twelve-branch brass chandelier hung garlands of greens, ribbons, pine cones and white feathers.

Angela whispered to Owen, "Do you think those are real angel feathers?"

"No. They're fake."

"Fake. Hmm. Too bad," she said.

Owen spied the receptionist and walked up. "Owen Michaels to see Sarah Parks," he said to the woman in her mid-fifties wearing a Christmas sweater and earrings in the shape of Christmas trees.

"Certainly. I'll announce you, Mr. Michaels."

The receptionist picked up the phone and relayed the information. "She'll be right out."

"Thanks." Owen walked back over to Angela who was observing several of the residents.

"This isn't heaven," Angela told him.

"This is where you used to live."

"No." She looked across the room.

In two Chippendale wing chairs upholstered in dark green velvet near a monstrous fireplace decorated with green garland, crystal lights, pine cones and enormous red bows, sat two well-dressed elderly women. The silver haired woman with a slight frame wore a simple pair of black slacks and a black sweater with rhinestone buttons. Her earrings sparkled in the twinkling lights. Her glasses hung around her neck from a gold chain. The woman next to her wore a long red and black plaid skirt with a red turtleneck sweater with a large panther shaped broach near her shoulder. Her hair was colored a beautiful auburn color that she wore chin length to show off very large stud earrings.

Angela did not know their earth age but they looked like the humans who passed to her 963-frequency home once their earth life was finished. However, both women did not look as if they were quite done with their earth experience. Angela wondered why they were here.

"Iris," the woman in the plaid skirt said. "You've repeated yourself three time. Do you know you're doing that?"

"No, Sherry. I don't know. And if I did, my kids would not have stuck me here."

"Well, don't get mad at me, Iris. The thing is. It's Christmas. And as lovely as the designers make this place, it's not the same as home used to be. Is it?"

"Do you think we're this way because our kids grew up and don't need us?"

Iris asked.

Sherry mused on this.

At that moment, a bicycle horn sounded disrupting the scene. An elderly woman dressed in garish pink and purple rode up on a scooter. She waved jauntily at Iris and Sherry. "Hello, girls!" She was bright and overly made-up. Not waiting for a response, the woman rode on.

"Gladys needs a stylist," Iris said.

Sherry turned to Iris. "Look at it this way, Iris. Gladys Handson is five years younger than we are and we can still walk. That's something."

"Yes, Sherry. Something to be thankful for."

Sherry folded her hands. "I have a lot of Christmas wishes this year. It takes me an hour to pray for the world."

"You, too?" Iris asked smiling. "You're a good person."

"And your friend."

The smiles between them created waves of energy that Angela was certain only she could see.

An erudite looking man in a camel wool jacket, black slacks and expensive looking shoes was reading a magazine upside down. As if feeling someone watching him, he raised his head, took off his tortoise-shell rimmed glasses and looked at Angela. She smiled at him for a very long moment. He smiled back at her and nodded his head.

The man's smile got brighter and wider and as it did, he looked younger.

Owen blinked, unsure of what he was seeing.

The man pinched the bridge of his nose, went back to his magazine, turned it right side up and began reading.

Angela turned to Owen. "I like it here."

"You do?"

Sarah Parks walked up. She was cheerful and poised in her navy blue business suit, stylish shoes and understated jewelry. She reached out to Owen.

"It's so nice to meet you, Mr. Michaels."

"My pleasure," he replied. "And you already know Angela."

Sarah turned her head and when her eyes met Angela, her mouth gaped, eyes widened and she froze. "I …I haven't had the pleasure. But, I would like to." She reached to shake Angela's hand.

Angela took both her hands and drew closer to Sarah. "Sarah. Sweet soul. You don't remember me?"

Sarah was confused. She looked to Owen. She looked back at Angela.

"I don't."

"No," Angela replied. "You couldn't. Could you?"

"Pardon?"

Angela looked around her at Iris. Sherry. Gladys. "This being earth and all. It would be impossible. The forgetting is massive."

"Forgetting? Ah!"

Sarah looked to Owen as if she'd readjusted. He got that. It happened a lot around Angela. He had yet to figure it out. Thank God the confusion she instilled with her attitude and answers to simple questions didn't last long. Frankly, he thought that Sarah having worked with dementia and Alzheimer patients would be used to the Angela's of the world.

He was more than flummoxed.

"Angela. I'm sorry, you said you were from heavenly…"

She interrupted. "It's all right, Owen. I'll be fine here."

Again, he was taken aback. Was he relieved to be rid of her? Or was this his reaction to missing her? He turned to Sarah. "If Angela isn't a resident here, how do we admit her? Or sign her in?"

"Owen. I don't actually have room for her."

"Well, that's not good."

While Owen was talking to Sarah about the business aspects, which did not appeal to her, she wandered over to Iris and Sherry who were still sitting in the Chippendale chairs. Iris looked up at her. Without saying a word, Angela put her heart hand on the top of Iris's head.

"What are you doing?" Iris asked.

"Shhh. It's a gift."

Angela closed her eyes for a short moment and then smiled. She lifted Iris's chin with her forefinger. "You are loved. You are never alone. Never separate. And all your wishes will come true."

Iris could only stare. "I choose to believe you."

"See that you do."

Angela then turned to Sherry. She put her hand on the top of Sherry's head. Then she pressed her forefinger into the middle of her forehead, between her eyes, just above the bridge of her nose. "Believe in those prayers."

"I do," Sherry said.

"I know you do. And that makes all the difference. You will have a lovely Christmas. And many more to come. Just as you dream them. Dream big. Never dream small. Will you do that?"

"Yes." Sherry smiled.

"Now continue sharing your stories with each other. Tell me about your children and grandchildren. What shall we wish for them for Christmas?"

"Oh, my!" Sherry put her hands to her cheeks. "I feel so different." She looked at her hands. "What's happening to me?"

Angela smiled. "Youth is in the mind."

"I've always said I was still a young woman." She touched her face which was radiant and glowing. She looked across at Iris. "Oh, my God, Iris. Look at you."

"What?"

"Our hands. Our faces. We are…"

Angela leaned close and whispered. "Tell the authorities here you are simply hydrated. Don't tell the truth. I've found truth on earth is not accepted."

"Oh, darlin'," Sherry said. "You got that right!"

Angela looked over to Owen who was deep in conversation with Sarah.

Iris leaned forward. "Who are you, dear?"

Angela knew her radiance of happiness was as bright as dawn rays. "I'm your new friend. I'm going to be staying with you all for a while." She looked at the group of people coming off the elevators to gather in the dining hall for lunch. Their faces were not old. Just hopeless. "Yes. I have some work to do here."

"I can tell you, darlin'," Iris said. "We will keep you busy."

"Oh, not that busy. You see, you all are willing. There is a difference," she said looking back to Owen.

"Sarah," Owen said. "What can I do?"

"As it happens, I have two residents who are vacationing for several months in Florida with their families. They would be happy to sub-let to you until they return."

"How long would that be?"

"The apartment is available only until February first. Legally, Angela can check herself out after seventy-two hours."

"This is a twist. I'd assumed that once you saw Angela, you might recognize her. I thought she might have forgotten her real name. Not that she even remembers her last name."

"It would help to know that," Sarah admitted.

"It would. Tell you what. The thing is my father had a heart attack. I have obligations back in Chicago and Angela simply appeared at our house last night. Clearly, she's not…uh…"

"Not an obvious Heavenly Acres resident?" She finished for him.

"Diplomatic. But yes."

Angela walked back to Owen and Sarah. She exuded happiness. "Owen, I would like to stay here for a bit."

Angela glanced back at Sherry and Iris then back to Sarah. "This is where I'm meant to be. For now."

Owen rocked back on his heels. "That's great. You look so happy."

"I am. It's so lovely here."

"Wonderful," Sarah said. "And how would you like to take care of her rent, Mr. Michaels?"

Owen searched Angela's happy face as she watched all the residents walk past her. He reached for his wallet, not sure if he was happy or reluctant to make the transaction.

* * * * *

Nine

When Owen drove up to his Dad's farmhouse, he saw Gregory sitting in a rocking chair on the front porch, blanket over his legs, mug in his hand, glaring at Owen as he parked and got out of the car.

"So, you did it?" Gregory barked.

"Took her home? I sure did."

Owen walked up the steps slowly remembering that the look on his father's face was the same as when he kicked a football through Mr. Stock's front window and the cost was over a hundred dollars. It took him a month of mowing the Stock's massive yard to pay off the debt. The purse of his dad's lips, the set to his jaw and the steely stare told Owen there was going to be hell to pay. And probably no reasoning with him at all.

"Well, in a manner of speaking that's what I did."

"Then speak clearly," Gregory demanded.

Owen leaned against the porch column and crossed his arms over his chest. The bitter cold air was nothing compared to the icy vibes his dad was spearing him with. "Apparently, they have no record of Angela No-Last-Name and the Administrator didn't recognize her either."

Gregory's expression softened. "That's not possible."

"Oh, it's possible."

"Frankly, I thought you were right. I just did not want her to go…quite yet." Gregory looked down at his cocoa. "Then where did she come from? Dressed in a night gown if not from Heavenly Acres?"

"I don't know. I called Quinn at the Sheriff's office to see if there were any missing persons matching her description. He ran preliminary checks. Nothing. He said he'd keep an eye out. Check with the Federal agencies and dig as much as he could. He promised he'd keep a watch out for me."

Gregory stared long into his cocoa mug. "Because you're leaving."

Owen braced. The ever-present battle was on again. "Dad. I have work. Julia."

"Sure."

"Look, I'm not going until the doctor checks you out tomorrow. If you're okay, you've got Holly and Sam who will be here at the snap of your fingers."

Owen pushed away from the column, went to his father and patted his shoulder. He crossed to the door and opened it and just as he stepped inside, he glanced back.

His father's head dropped to his chest as he said lowly, but loud enough for Owen to hear, "But they aren't family."

Admittedly, Owen felt like a heel. But he'd made promises to Julia. Not to mention paperwork he absolutely had to get to his clients by the day after Christmas for them to make charity contributions before New Year's Eve. They depended on Owen. He had always been there for him. He took his job seriously because it was very serious work.

The only problem was that his father didn't see it that way.

He took off his overcoat and just as he reached up to hang it on the hook, Beau came bounding in. He hovered against Owen's leg to receive the cursory pet.

"Hello, boy. How're ya doin'?"

Beau did not linger for another pet. Instead, he went to the door and stood rigid. The door opened and Gregory walked in.

"Beau. Come to see me, huh?" Greg petted Beau, glanced at Owen and said, "I'm making more cocoa. You want some?"

"Sure," Owen said.

Owen watched as Gregory shuffled down the hall. But Beau did not follow as he always did. Instead, Beau went back to the door, rigid again as if waiting for something.

Or someone.

Beau looked back at Owen holding his stare for a long moment. The dog turned back to the door. Then he looked back at Owen.

Owen swiped his hand through his hair as revelation hit him. "She's not coming back, Beau."

Beau barked. Then he turned back to the door and laid down.

"Angela's gone, boy," Owen said, wondering why the Golden Retriever was acting so strangely. Did the dog know something he didn't?

Owen heard his dad rustling in the kitchen. "You need help, Dad?" Owen asked walking away from the door.

Beau didn't move. He kept his eyes on the closed door.

* * * * *

Angela had been elated when Sarah told her that she'd be seated with Iris, Sherry and Gladys at all their meals. She had looked forward to spending more time with them and she hoped they would introduce her to the rest of the residents. She liked the formal arrangements for the evening meal.

Iris told her that the white cloth was cut short rather than long so as not to interfere with scooters and walkers that some of the residents used to stay ambulatory. Angela had frowned. Humans had legs. They only needed some adjustments to correct their balance and gait. Angela thought that an easy task compared to the direct mission she'd been given by the Celestial Council of Light of Twenty-Four.

As the waiters poured water and caffeine free tea, Angela looked around the festive room with the tiny poinsettias on each table and candles with flames she couldn't extinguish. Sherry explained the candles were battery operated. Whatever that was. It had something to do with Fire Marshall Laws. Angela didn't know about those laws, either.

The waiter brought their plates. Angela stared at the food on the plate. It looked like a swirl of white ribbons with dots of green and red. She looked at the waiter. "I like cocoa."

"In the morning," the middle-aged man with sparse grey hair said.

Angela waited while everyone was served. She had no idea how to grasp the strange looking food. She was aware of the pangs in the middle of her body that now were making noise in addition to causing a great deal of discomfort.

She noticed that Gladys held a Bible in her lap and with her head bowed she was praying. Most of the prayers Angela knew. But she'd never experienced the passages cobbled together in the way that Gladys did, turning the pages without a theme to follow, she read half a thought, flipped through more pages and read something else. It made no sense at all. Sherry and Iris were indulgent.

Sherry whispered, "We let Gladys say her prayers in this manner that seems to please her."

"That's very kind of you."

Iris nodded. "And our food is always cold when she finishes. Not good for the digestion." Iris reached over and touched Gladys's hand. "Gladys, you can stop praying now. God heard you."

"You can never be sure," Gladys replied.

"God hears everything," Angela assured her.

Gladys slammed the book shut, picked up her fork and spoon and began twirling the pasty ribbons around with the help of the spoon. She spoke not another word to Angela or the others.

"What is the food?" Angela asked.

"Fettuccine Alfredo. It has sun tried tomatoes and peas. The pasta is gluten-free," Iris smiled.

"It's tasteless, if you ask me. It needs more Parmesan cheese, basil and grilled chicken to make me happy." Sherry took two bites of the food and sat back. "I used to make the best Southern creamed corn with bacon fat and real whipping cream. Now that was good eating."

"I met Burt Lancaster once," Gladys said without further explanation.

Sherry and Iris ignored Gladys.

Angela tried to swirl the fettuccini around with the fork and spoon and failed. She could barely get the pasta to her mouth. When she chewed it, she wondered why humans would want this food and not the delicious cocoa Owen had made for her.

"What do you think?"

"I like cocoa." Angela replied which drew chuckles from all three of her table mates.

"It's downright a sin not to put garlic in Italian dishes," Sherry said. "My mother was an excellent cook. God rest her soul."

Angela brightened. "Oh, she's not resting. She's in a French cuisine class now."

The three women didn't miss a beat and didn't ask for further comment from Angela.

"It seems to me," Iris said, "… that if God hears everything, then why doesn't he just take us instead of making us live with all these whackos."

"I met Ernest Borgnine, too," Gladys said. "He was a lovely man."

Iris leaned toward Angela. "See what I mean, Angela?"

"I do. This time I'll be more focused," Angela replied.

Iris's painted-on eyebrows rose. "This time?"

"I was distracted by Owen when I first touched you."

Gladys sat up straight suddenly aware of the conversation. "Owen? Is that the handsome young man who brought you?"

"Gladys, hush," Sherry said. "Now do that thing to me again."

Angela reached over to Sherry and placed her palm on her forehead. She closed her eyes and breathed deeply. She held her breath for nearly a minute and then exhaled for almost as long. To anyone passing by the table, they wouldn't think anything out of the ordinary was happening---until Angela lowered her hand.

Sherry's eyes popped open. Gone was the rheumy, cataract cloud that had partially covered Sherry's eyes. Her skin looked brighter, uplifted and free of age spots.

Iris dropped her fork.

Gladys gaped and threw her palm over her mouth.

Angela smiled at Sherry. "How do you feel?"

"Light." She rubbed her elbow. And then her left knee. "And the pain is gone." She put her hands around her neck. "It's not stiff."

"What did you do?" Gladys' gasped.

"I re-aligned her energies. It wasn't badly mis-aligned, thank goodness."

Iris stared at Sherry. "You continue to look younger by each breath."

"And I feel it, too," Sherry replied.

"Do it to me," Gladys said putting her Bible on the table.

"Of course," Angela replied and placed her palm on Gladys' forehead. She closed her eyes. She could feel Gladys' transformation taking place. The woman had a severely blocked third eye chakra which made sense to Angela. Gladys probably had never heard of chakras, breath work or clearing energies.

"This is amazing," Iris said. "They both look years younger than they did when we sat down to dinner. Please. Could you do the same to me, Angela?"

"I will."

Angela repeated the same procedure, though she breathed even more deeply since Iris had memory blockages going back to her infancy. She dropped her hand.

Gladys was mesmerized as she watched Iris transform in front of her. "Was it a special prayer you said? I need to know. I must be doing it wrong."

"All prayers are special if the intention is meant with love."

Iris held her fingers to her temples. Her eyes flitted from one woman to the other. "My thoughts are so clear and so is my eyesight."

"So are mine," Sherry said. "I feel like I have my right mind back."

All three looked at Angela with admiration and gratitude. "Thank you, Angela," Iris said.

"Yes, we are deeply grateful," Gladys chimed. "But tell us. What's the secret?"

Angela's smile was mega-watt brilliant. "Hope."

"So, by our feeling pain-free, lighter and looking younger, we think younger."

"And we feel like we can do more. Be more," Iris joined Sherry's comments.

The three women compared experiences among themselves, as Angela noticed other diners gazing over at their table. They were pointing fingers, gasping in disbelief, and smiling.

Angela rose and went to the table next to hers. "May I help you as well?" she asked.

"Oh, please!" The woman with the silver hair tugged on Angela's arm. "Does it hurt?"

"What you have done all your life is painful. Wouldn't a change of heart and thinking be called for now?" Angela asked her.

All three table mates begged Angela to "transform" them. It didn't take Angela long to work on four tables of four each. Women and men had the same results. They felt happier, younger and pain free. One man closed his walker and carried it away from the table when he left. Another woman had been quite stooped due to a thirty-year back injury. She was not completely upright when she rose from the table, but she was vastly straighter. She was profuse in her thanks and gratitude.

Angela told them all, she needed no thanks. She asked them to give their thanks to God.

*****

Ten

Owen had given up his suit and tie after taking Angela to Heavenly Acres. He found an old high school sweatshirt, a pair of warm jogging pants and white athletic socks he must have worn when he played basketball at the town YMCA during summers after work on the farm.

Sitting on the bed with Beau curled up at his feet, Owen was surprised how comfortable he felt working on his laptop, late at night in the silent house. His dad had gone to bed hours earlier.

Owen checked on him every half hour, surprising himself how concerned he truly was about his dad's health. He had to admit that he'd been in a slight state of shock of his own over the heart attack. It had scared the bejesus out of him. In these quiet hours he'd faced the one fact he'd turned away from for a long time.

"Dad is the only family I've got."

The chaos, and that is what it felt like to Owen, over the Angela issue, had steered his focus away from his dad and onto her. She had shown up at the precise moment that Owen had wanted to have his dad all to himself.

The thought was a revelation to him. His behavior portrayed the opposite. He and Gregory had been bickering since the day his mother died. Owen had gone to Chicago to make a new life because he didn't want to be on the farm and give up his career as an estate planner. He loved what he did. The satisfaction he derived from helping others was most likely equivalent to the joy his father got from being a dairy farmer.

As Owen looked back on his younger years, he'd liked the farm chores. Some he loved.

"It wasn't the work," he finally admitted to himself.

He had to face the fact that if his Dad passed, he would inherit the farm. Sure, he could sell it, but something rattled inside him. He could no more sell the family land than fly.

Perhaps Sam and Holly would stay on and run it for him.

He looked up at the night sky through the open window. It was clear and the stars were unusually bright.

Beau perked up, looked up at the window as well. He jumped off the bed and went to the window.

Beau barked.

Owen put the laptop aside and got up. "What is it, Beau? Do you see someone outside?"

Owen leaned down to pet Beau, but when he stood and gazed at the sky, this time he saw what Beau saw.

An orb of multicolored lights swirled around one particular star. That star appeared to move closer. As it did, the colors flashed and grew in intensity.

"What in the world?"

Beau barked again. Owen put his hand on Beau's head to reassure him. "It's okay---I think."

Owen had never seen a UFO, alien or spaceship, but at this point in the earth's timeline, he'd expect just about anything.

The swirling rainbow moved closer to the farm. It hovered over the top of the hill where he and his dad had found Angela. It swept back and forth like a pendulum and then it began moving to the northwest.

Beau barked twice more.

"Shhh! Beau. Don't wake Dad."

Both Owen and Beau watched the lights as it traveled down the hill away from the farm.

"It's going in the direction of Heavenly Acres," Owen said. "My God. What is it?"

Owen went to his laptop and searched the web news for any reports of strange rainbow light sightings. Nothing. He then called his friend, Quinn, at the Sheriff's Office. Quinn told him there were no reports, but he'd take Owen's notes.

Beau was riveted to the scene outside the window, but the lights were gone. A light snow fell and the stars had disappeared behind clouds. Owen watched Beau.

He knew what Beau was feeling. Sensing.

He stroked Beau's head. "You miss her, doncha, boy? Strangely, I kinda do, too."

* * * * *

The next morning, Angela was up early. After saying her prayers of gratitude for the instructions she'd received during the night from the celestial council, all she could think about as she put on a pair of Kris' jeans and a pretty blue sweater and sneakers, was the hot cocoa she would have that morning at the dining table.

She walked downstairs rather than taking the elevator since she didn't know how to use one. She saw a line of six cars under the portico. Curious, she went toward the door, then heard her name being called.

"Oh, Angela!" Iris called. "There you are! I went to your room but you were already down here. It's so exciting!"

"What is?"

"Last night I called my son and daughter-in-law and told them all about what happened. We talked till almost midnight. They could tell how clear brained I was now. I sent them a selfie and they were shocked! They drove all the way from Milwaukee last night to bring me home for Christmas. They want me to stay for New Year's, too!" Iris hugged Angela. "It's a miracle. You are a miracle."

"No, Iris. The miracle was within you. You just must believe."

"Yes. That's what Christmas is all about, isn't it? Believing." Iris beamed the joy of a truly happy person.

Iris left with her son and daughter-in-law just as two young children came scampering into the building.

"Do you work here?" The little girl of about seven asked.

"No."

"Oh. We came to get my grandma Gladys and take her home with us," the boy announced. "She's all cured now and she can go to my baseball games this spring and watch me play. She said she wasn't going to miss a single one."

"That's right," the little girl said. "Daddy put us in the car last night and we drove here from Nashville. Mommy's going to have a big family Christmas dinner she said. Just like we used to."

Gladys walked down the stairs.

Angela turned and was wide eyed. "Gladys. No scooter?"

"I'm donating it to Heavenly Acres. Thanks to you, I have my life back. I have my family."

"Family. Yes," Angela mused, not certain these emotions humans had about family could be so profoundly loving. She didn't feel that about Owen and Gregory. Yet.

Gladys embraced Angela. "Help the others, Angela. Give them what you gave us. Bye for now. And Merry Christmas."

A few moments later, Angela said goodbye to Sherry when her family came in two SUV's they called their large automobiles. They were moving Sherry out of Heavenly Acres and back home for good. Angela's inner knowing told her that all the others would have similar plans before the year turned new.

She stood on the portico and waved to everyone as they left. She looked up to the second story window and without being beckoned, she knew she had more work to do.

Angela walked into George Schultz's room and was assaulted with the smell of lost hope. Across the room in a large upholstered chair sat a woman wrapped in an old thick sweater and a blanket.

"Hello, George." Angela walked over to the hospital bed that had been erected in George's room. Gladys had told Angela that this kind of bed was brought in when a person was in Hospice. He had only days to live according to Gladys.

"Who are you?" the sickly man asked.

"I'm Angela. Gladys sent me."

"Oh. You're the healer. Well, you should know, I'm not like the others."

Angela laid her palm on George's forehead. It was filled with black ice from not having been used in his lifetime. She put her other palm over his crown. It, too, was cold. No love coming in or going out. She withdrew her hands.

She shouldn't have been surprised that there was no transformation.

"Why do you say you're different than the others?"

"I have no family."

"You can be my family," Angela offered.

"No, I can't," he replied. "You're a spirit. You don't have family."

Angela took a step back. "How do you know that?"

"I'm dying. I'm between the worlds. I've been to your world. Earth and this life are the dream. Your heaven world is reality."

He took a shallow breath, then pointed across the room. "See Bess over there?"

"Yes."

"She needs your help. She has a son. He will come get her."

Angela looked at the elderly woman, hugging the blanket around her stooped shoulders. Lost hope clung to every inch of her.

"Hello, Bess," Angela said walking toward the woman. "Tell me about your son. Where does he live?"

"A long way. Detroit. He's very busy with his concrete business."

Angela put her hand on Bess's forehead. Then the other hand on her crown. She closed her eyes and concentrated.

"Detroit is not so far. India is long way away. And besides, it's just a few miles."

"I want you to stand up, Bess."

"Why?"

"I will hug you."

Bess stood up. Angela dropped the blanket and hugged Bess tight until her stooped back straightened while Angela held her. "I want you to think about your son. He will be happy to see you for Christmas."

"I don't want to be a burden."

"Bess, you tell him you will cook for him. Shop. Wrap presents. He will take you to the Christmas concert."

"How do you know about that?"

"His angel told me."

Bess sat back down, surprised how her movements were painless. "This is incredible. George. Look!"

"I'm looking, Bess. You're getting younger."

George looked at Angela. "When I get to heaven, are all the angels as beautiful as you? Inside and out?"

"Yes."

Angela turned to Bess. "You go to your room and call your son."

"Oh, I will!" Bess jumped up, surprising them all. She went to George's bed. "Merry Christmas, George. Thank you for this."

"Don't thank me, thank the angel," he said.

Bess's eyes were filled with tears of gratitude when she looked at Angela. "I should have guessed. Thank you," she choked out the words and put her hand over her heart. She said no more.

When Bess left the room, Angela turned to George. "I was told it's your time to go home. Are you ready?"

"I am," he sighed.

Angela put her palm on his eyes as he shut them. She put the other hand on his heart. "You are a good soul. Sleep with the angels, George."

She waited a few minutes.

George took his last breath as a human.

Angela left the room quietly.

* * * * *

Eleven

Winter dawn could be blinding, Owen thought, as he walked over the glittering new-fallen snow toward the cow barn. The air was still, crisp but not blisteringly cold. There was a peace that only winter morning in the country could bring. He'd heard a rooster crow earlier and now the cows mooing. But the silence of this farm was something he'd forgotten. In the silence one could measure their own thoughts. Reflect on beauty which he seldom if ever had time to do in his life. But in his past, he'd walked these pastures and country roads often. He'd named his favorite trees and measured the height weekly of the sunflowers he and his mother had planted along the drive. Life had been different then.

But then---that was childhood. Wasn't that what being a child was supposed to be?

He lifted his face to the warm sun. He patted his too tight high school sweatshirt pockets for sunglasses. It was an automatic gesture. This plaid wool jacket was his dad's. His sunglasses was another thing he'd forgotten in the flurry of panic and shock when he'd left Chicago. He didn't remember locking his door and had to call the superintendent to go up and double check that he had.

Thank God security, locking doors and cars were rote for him. Another city-living lesson he'd learned early on. He'd lived in an old apartment building in Wrigleyville only a month when his apartment had been broken into. He owned very little at the time, but his new out-of-the-box flat screen television had been too enticing for—somebody. The thief was never found. However, Owen had learned from his neighbors that putting the new television box out for the trash had alerted a neighbor, or passer-by that in the small building was a new television. Owen had thought about going door-to-door to announce his presence to his neighbors and check out their apartments for his television. He'd visited only three people, nice people, when he gave up the ghost. Of course, the fact that he worked eighty plus hours a week to make a name for himself in the finance firm nixed any plans for watching football or basketball. He only hoped to catch an at home Cubs game or two during the season. It never happened.

Owen tromped into the cow barn and found the entire Kane family hard at work. Sam was laying out feed. Mary filled the water troughs with a hose. Holly handed Owen a pitch fork.

"I'm going up to the house to fix breakfast for Greg," she said. "Did you have breakfast, Owen?"

"Breakfast?"

Holly cocked her head and grinned. "Do you know what it is?"

"The meal I skip?"

"I figured as much."

"Sometimes a smoothie," he offered with an embarrassed smile.

Mary and Joe giggled. Mary shot them a warning look. They went back to work.

"What did you have yesterday for breakfast?"

He looked down, toed the hay covered cement floor. "Some of your Shepherd's pie around noon-ish."

"Well," she said, pushing up her jacket sleeves. "I have my work cut out for me, don't I?" She walked sternly out of the barn.

Owen turned to Sam. "She is so like my mom, it's spooky."

"Yeah. I kinda picked that up from Greg," Sam chuckled. "The kids and I know never to cross Holly. Isn't that right, kids?"

Mary turned off the water. Joe finished scooping feed from the back of the trailer into a large bucket. "Yep!" They laughed in unison.

Joe jumped down off the trailer. "Mom's the general. We're the army. It works."

Owen stifled a chuckle as Sam slapped his shoulder playfully. "You'll get used to it. Listen, I gotta take the tractor out and get more feed. Owen? You got this?"

"I do." Owen rubbed his hands together. "But if not, the kids will show me."

Joe gave his dad a thumbs up. "Yes, we will!"

Mary rolled her eyes and looked pleadingly at her father.

"What?" Owen asked. "You think I can't do this?" He shoved up his sleeves.

Joe, always the one who was short on words, but just as inquisitive as Mary asked, "You go to a city gym, huh?"

Mary pointed to Owen's upper arms. "Those."

"Uh..."

Joe interrupted. "My dad doesn't need to go to a gym."

Owen's mouth quirked into a sideways grin. "Apparently." Joe didn't need to say anything more. To this boy, Owen had a soft job and his father's well-defined muscular physique was earned by physical labor. Sam was natural. Owen was synthetic. Was that where Joe was going with this?

Owen reached for the big bucket of feed with one hand. The sucker had to weigh fifty pounds, but Owen wasn't going to wince. "Where to?"

Joe pointed to the end of the line of cows. "Down there. Then up on the other side. Those guys need a lot."

By the time Owen got to the end of the line, he was glad he had pushed himself at the gym the last month. Just so he didn't embarrass himself in front of a seven-year-old and a nine-year-old.

Mary helped scoop the feed out of Owen's bucket. "So how come you took Angela away?"

I thought so. Here it comes. Dad probably programmed them. "I didn't."

"Yes, you did," Mary countered.

"Mom told us," Joe added.

"What did she tell you? Exactly?"

"That you didn't like her. That Angela was too strange for you. That…"

Owen raised his palm in the air. "Okay. I get it."

Mary shook her head and put the scoop down. "No, you don't!" She said firmly.

Owen blinked. Mary had all the makings of a trial lawyer. "Excuse me?"

Joe stepped closer. "I think I wanna stay a kid forever. Except for the biceps."

"Why's that?" Owen asked.

"Because adults are off the charts clueless." Joe replied with his hands on his hips.

"Yeah," Mary chimed in. "Clueless."

No question about it. Kids knew how to gang up on the third wheel. Even worse, he was guilty as accused. Clueless. "I don't follow."

"Angela *was* different. Good different. Couldn't you see it?"

"What? That she was....uh."

"She wasn't sick," Mary explained in a lilting tone as if she were talking to the ignoramus now. "She didn't need special care. We have a cousin who is special needs and she IS special. But Angela..."

Joe watched Owen intently. "You never saw it, did you?" Mary started to speak, but Joe gave her the "shut up" look. She shook him off. "How Angela glows. Not like us. But in colors all around her."

"Yeah," Joe affirmed. "She's a diamond."

Owen let their words sink in. "A.... diamond."

Joe sighed. "That's what I thought."

"Me, too. You don't see it." Mary agreed.

Owen had no idea what they were talking about. He'd seen a radiance in Angela, born of her beauty but that was all. If there was some kind of rainbow light around her, he'd truly missed it.

Rainbow light.

He remembered the strange lights he and Beau had seen in the sky the night before. Did Angela have something to do with that kaleidoscopic phenomenon? By the time he went to sleep, he'd chalked the whole incident up to some kind of Northern Lights incident. It wouldn't be the first time he'd seen Northern Lights in the Wisconsin winter skies. There was always an explanation for everything. He'd have to dig into it further. But what could a swirl of rainbow lights have to do with Angela?

Sam drove the tractor back into the barn with more feed.

"Hey, guys. Let's finish this up. Mom says breakfast is ready. And I don't want those veggie omelets and biscuits to get cold."

"We're on it," Owen said as he took his empty bucket back to the trailer to fill it up. Holly made them breakfast. The same identical breakfast that was his favorite growing up on the farm.

Have I come home or entered the twilight zone?

* * * * *

Twelve

Owen washed the breakfast dishes while Holly, Sam and the kids went out to the milking parlor. He complimented Holly on the biscuits which were as light as the ones his mother used to make. Since he had a good deal of work yet to do, he went to his room and powered up his laptop.

Spreading out his files on the bed, he made several business calls each of which led to other calls. He downloaded several corporate earnings charts and emailed them to clients.

His dad came to his bedroom open door and tapped the door jamb. Owen looked up to see his father dressed in dark green corduroy slacks, a green sweater and his camel jacket and winter boots. "Did you forget my appointment today?"

Owen glanced at his watch. "Holy….I did. I'll throw on some clothes and meet you in the living room. Gimme five minutes."

"Yeah. You can shave later," Gregory groaned and walked away.

* * * *

Dr. Ellis' nurse took Gregory's pulse, blood pressure, temperature and ran a new EKG. When Dr. Ellis came into the room, he wasn't smiling.

"Everything okay, Doc?" Gregory asked.

"You're looking good, Greg. I do want you to rest. No stress. No activity except for a walk every day, but not too far." He looked at Owen. "You should go with him."

"Are you concerned?" Owen asked.

"Precaution is the best medicine," Doctor Ellis said.

Owen's suspicion was that the good Doctor was not telling them everything they should know.

After listening to Gregory's heart, the doctor told him to put his shirt back on and that he would see him in a week.

As the doctor left, Owen said, "You finish getting dressed. I have to go to the bathroom."

"Yeah, sure you do. Tell Doc I said Merry Christmas."

Owen hadn't fooled his dad one bit.

He left the room and was fortunate to stop Dr. Ellis before he saw the next patient. 'Dr. Ellis. I need to know whatever there is I need to know."

Dr. Ellis exhaled deeply. "It was a mild heart attack, but his heart is weaker than I'd like. What concerns me is his lack of will to fight."

"That's a concern?"

"Owen, loss of the will to thrive kills more people than disease." He put his hand on Owen's shoulder. "I'm glad you're here."

Doctor Ellis went into the next examining room.

"No pressure there," he mumbled to himself.

* * * * *

Owen heated a pot of water and made two mugs of tea with honey and took them into the living room where his dad was resting.

Gregory sat in his overstuffed chair, his eyes glued to the unlit Christmas tree, still bare of ornaments. "You know your mom used to decorate a gorgeous tree. Remember?"

Owen handed Gregory a mug of tea and sipped his. "I do. I barely remember an ornament that we didn't make ourselves."

Owen walked to the back of the tree and plugged in the lights. He stepped back. The old-fashioned colored lights had to be thirty years old but they all worked. Funny. There wasn't an ornament on the tree but there was magic in the tree that he and his father had planted decades ago. The colored lights were reflected around the room by the big mirror on the wall which had been strategically placed by his mother for the exact purpose of doubling Christmas tree lights.

What happened to those ornaments?" Owen asked.

"Rotted. Like me."

"Dad. You are not rotted," Owen countered.

"Yeah?"

"Not in the least. You're gonna heal."

"And you're gonna leave."

"Dad."

Owen didn't want to fall into another argument that would never end. He looked over at Beau who was still waiting by the front door. "What is he doing? She's not coming back."

Gregory put his hands on his chest and looked at Beau.

"Yes, she is. She said she would."

Owen's head fell back. His frustration over the Angela issue was climbing to new heights by the hour. "Dad. She's impaired. At best. She thinks…Oh, never mind."

Gregory rose from the chair. "I should be off to bed."

"You want any help?"

"No, son. I'm fine." He walked over to Beau who was still waiting by the front door. "Good night, Beau."

Beau didn't look up or follow Gregory to bed. He stared at the door.

Owen watched his father walk down the hall, go to his room, and leave the door ajar in case Beau changed his mind. Owen looked over at Beau.

He went to the door and opened it. Without saying a word to the dog, Beau got up and walked onto the front porch.

The night was clear and the air frosty. Owen hugged himself and looked above the trees to the stars. Beau leaned against his leg and Owen stroked his head and ears for a long time.

"I wonder how she's doing, Beau."

Beau whimpered a response.

"I know. I think the kids are right. She's different. Special. I wonder if I was wrong about her."

Beau barked.

"I figured you'd agree."

Owen turned. "C'mon."

They went inside.

* * * * *

CHICAGO.

Three massive contemporary Venetian glass chandeliers lit the upscale North Shore restaurant where Julia and her friends were celebrating the design company's Christmas party. Julia wore a cherry red sequined, low-cut dress as she dangled her fifteen-hundred-dollar high heeled shoe off her foot from a high bar stool in the center of the barroom. The company had taken over the bar area for pre-dinner drinks and the much anticipated bonus checks. The bonus was distributed according to one's value and performance with the company.

Julia had yet to have her boss and company owner assess and review her work at the Yacht Club. That was tomorrow, so she hadn't been sure if she'd even get a check at all.

It sat in front of her inside an un-opened heavy cream-colored stationary envelope. She liked the gold wax seal on the back.

Details. Always the details.

"So, where's Owen?" Tallulah inquired.

"Working late," Julia evaded. "You know how it is. Year end and all."

"Oh," Tallulah slapped her over-ringed hand on the table top. "Workaholic." She took another sip of her martini leaving a dark ruby red lipstick smear on the large bowl-shaped glass.

Tallulah was as dramatic as her name. She over-killed everything. Her long black crepe dress with chiffon sleeves was almost backless. She wore three strings of pearls down her back to show off her greatest asset. For some reason, her drama appealed to a great many clients. She was said to be the biggest bonus winner every year.

"You haven't opened your bonus," Gerald, the accounting manager, observed. He was sixty years old and counting the days to his retirement. He spent his off-time looking at beach houses and condos from one end of North America to the other.

Julia couldn't help thinking Gerald was only interested in her reaction to her check. *Not a good sign. Maybe the envelope is empty.*

"I thought you said Owen had to go to his father's farm," Gerald said. "He's working from there or is it the cows?"

Tallulah put down her glass. "Call him. Tell him to get his butt down here. We'll be dancing till midnight!"

Julia took her cell phone out of her retro jewel-encrusted evening bag. She punched in Owen's number.

Owen answered on the first ring.

"Owen! Our friends are asking why you're hanging with the cows and not with us?" She smiled over at Tallulah who winked back.

"That's not exactly true, Julia. My dad is recuperating."

"And how's that going, dear?"

"Uh, slow, actually."

Julia held her breath. Taking her envelope and evening bag, she slid off the bar stool and walked to the side of the bar for more privacy. "Slow? What exactly are you saying, Owen?"

"It's complicated."

Julia clenched her jaw. She spoke slowly. "No. It's not at all. He's either better like you said and you're coming back here tomorrow or there's something else."

"Julia. It's my dad."

"Yes. And *my* father expects you back here for the gala and Christmas. Perhaps I should explain to you. This isn't just a party. My father has spent weeks---months talking you up to his friends and his most valued clients. He has done this because I told him this is about *my* future as well as yours. We are both helping you, Owen."

"I didn't know all that. To that degree. Tell you what. I'll give him a call."

"And say what?"

"I'll explain that I'm trying to make it there. I really am."

"I'm glad to hear it. Goodbye, Owen."

Her hand shook so much it took three punches to end the call. Owen was being evasive and that wasn't like him. Something was wrong. Yes. His father was ill, but if there was something dire, wouldn't Owen simply tell her the truth? Something wasn't right at all. If Owen had been one of her exes, she'd suspect another woman. But he was on a dairy farm for goodness' sake.

The one thing Julia knew was that her Spidey antennae didn't go on alert when there were not grounds for suspicion.

Never.

* * * *

Owen sat on his bed with Beau. He'd closed up his laptop and moved the files to the bedside table. Beau looked up at him and cocked his head.

"I know. Julia can be a pickle."

He ruffled Beau's ears, then kissed his forehead. "You are the best dog. I'm glad you're here with dad."

The ringing of his cell phone nearly made him jump. "Oh, no."

Thinking it was Julia again, he looked at the caller ID. "Heavenly Acres. At this time of night? What in the world?"

"Hello."

"Mr. Michaels. This is Sarah at Heavenly Acres."

"Yes, what can I do for you?"

"For one thing, you can come pick up your Angela. She's checked herself out. She says she wants to come home."

"Home?" Owen's voice squeaked with surprise.

"With you and Mr. Michaels. First thing in the morning will do."

Owen swiped his cheek. "Has she done anything wrong?"

"That would be putting it mildly. She's cost me a fortune."

Owen shot to his feet. "How much damage are we talking? What did she break?"

"She didn't break anything. My residents are leaving. Cancelling their contracts. They're not coming back after their holidays with their families. Their families claim they don't need us anymore."

Owen was flummoxed. "I don't understand what Angela has to do with this."

He could hear Sarah sigh over the phone. "They tell me she gave them hope."

* * * * *

Thirteen

Angela dutifully fastened her seat restraint in Owen's car after he put her bag with his mother's clothes Gregory had lent her in the back seat. His energies were vibrating on a very low frequency that she'd not experienced from any human she'd met thus far on earth. She wondered if this was what Angel B-2222 referred to as anger.

He started the car and drove out onto the country road. They passed forested areas with snow hugging the bare brown limbs and wide expanses of snow-covered pasture land. Homes were decorated with garlands and wreaths. Bows of red and silver and gold. It was lovely how artistic humans could be.

She was exhilarated over her success with the people at Heavenly Acres. What a fulfilling assignment that part had been. She'd have to remember to sign up for that mission again. Experiencing their happiness was all the reward she needed.

She glanced at Owen. The set to his jaw was hard and stern. He gripped the round apparatus in front of him he used to stay in his seat, she guessed. She thought it odd he was silent.

"It is so white. So lovely here. Is it like this all the time? Throughout your year time, I mean."

"No."

"I hadn't imagined the beauty would be this majestic."

Owen cricked his stiff neck. It cracked. "And obviously, that's because you're from someplace else."

"I am."

"Then why don't you tell me about it. Because right now, you've upset the entire administrative staff at Heavenly Acres, not to mention me and my father."

"Everything will be all right," she assured him.

"You know I hate it when people say that," he grumbled.

"Why? It is the truth."

"It's seldom the truth."

"Only people with little faith say that."

"And you have lots of it, I suppose," he snorted at her like a horse.

She was right to guess that he was angry. She would have to negate that vibration and turn it to positivism and fast. "I do. And you will, too. Quite soon."

"See? That's just it. You say these cryptic things and you make me..."

"What," she smiled as she interrupted him.

He hit the round apparatus. "Nuts! You make me crazy. I should go to Heavenly Acres."

"It's very nice there," she smiled at him again.

"Ugh!"

When they arrived at the farm house, Gregory was waiting at the front door. Beau ran down the steps and straight up to Angela. She squatted down and hugged Beau.

Beau licked her cheek. "I knew you'd come back."

"I missed you, Beau. You are the only one I can communicate with telepathically."

"It was no picnic here, either."

Owen went to the back seat and got the plaid tote carrying his mother's clothes his father had loaned to Angela and a brown grocery sack.

Gregory stretched out his arms to hug Angela as she came up the steps. "Angela! I am so glad you are back!"

"I missed you, too. But those people needed me," She whispered.

"So do we," Gregory whispered back.

Owen walked up the steps. "Dad. I picked up some heart healthy meals on the way back."

Gregory frowned at the sack. "I was hoping for pizza."

Beau barked.

Angela's eyes shot to Gregory. "What's pizza? And why does Beau like it?"

Gregory put his finger to his lips. "Shh. Don't tell my doctor."

Owen opened the door. "I didn't hear that," he had to chuckle at his irascible father.

* * * * *

While Gregory grabbed Beau's leash off the wall peg, Owen took off his coat. Angela took the food to the kitchen. Owen entered the kitchen and went immediately to work setting the table. Gregory hooked the leash to Beau's collar and walked to the back kitchen door and opened it.

"Dad? Where are you going?"

"My doctor ordered me to walk every day. Right? So, Beau is my companion. Besides, he gets bored hanging around here all the time."

As Greg left, Angela pulled out the cocoa mugs. "Could you make your cocoa for me? They gave me cocoa at Heavenly Acres, but it was..."

"Awful. Probably from a package."

She was standing under the cupboard where the cocoa and sugar were stored. Owen reached over and around her. His face was close to hers. Gone was the lower energy field she'd picked up earlier. He lingered a long moment as if he wanted to be close to her, but she didn't know why. His vibratory frequency rose so much she could see pink light coming from his heart. She knew this light of love. Angels used it often for healing bodies and souls.

He held the cocoa in front of her.

"No. It wasn't your cocoa."

"I have a secret ingredient," he said softly still not moving away from her. His face was so close to hers; she was certain their lips could touch.

"It is love?"

"Love?" He blinked as if he were unscrambling his thoughts. "Uh, no. Honey."

"Like what your father puts on his scone?" she asked, her eyes peered into his. She looked deeply—down to his soul. He had so much love inside him. She had not seen this much love since…

"BOY!"

The back door flew open and Gregory burst in. "It's cold out there."

Beau raced into the room and went straight to his water bowl and slurped up half the contents.

Owen self-consciously moved quickly away from Angel and when he did, she felt a rift crack through the energy field they had created. She didn't understand exactly what had just happened, but she knew that one moment they were creating love and the next it was gone. She looked down at Beau.

Beau lifted his head. Telepathically, he said, "Sorry, for the interruption, Angela. Owen was about to kiss you."

"Kiss?"

"I'll explain later," Beau replied.

Owen moved reluctantly away from Angela.

She noticed that Owen nervously spilled the cocoa and the sugar as he began making the magic mixture. He poured in the milk and searched for the marshmallows. "We're out of marshmallows?"

Gregory looked up. "Oh, Holly brought some over this morning. They're in the pantry."

"Good deal." He turned on the stove. "How was the walk, Dad?"

"Beau liked it. Invigorating, I guess. I'm hungry!" He grinned widely.

"So are we," Owen said side-glancing at Angela.

She did not miss the gaze he sent her. She felt a zing go through her physical body. She would have to ask the medical team on The Other Side about these sensations she was having when she was near Owen. None of this had been part of her downloads or instructions. She wondered how they could have missed something that was growing in intensity. These "feelings" she heard the women at Heavenly Acres talk about; were they common to humans? Angels had compassion. They had unconditional love for all living beings and things. But some of these emotions, Iris dubbed them, created pangs in her heart and belly. She had said they were sadness and grief. These were the pains that Gregory endured every day from what she could see. He felt separated from Kris and his parents even though she knew he communicated with their spirits.

Perhaps it was different for humans not being able to touch another's physical body. She knew she liked it when Gregory hugged her. And she'd definitely felt elated and strong vibrations of happiness when Iris, Gladys and Sherry hugged her goodbye.

What perplexed her now was the strong magnetic pull between her and Owen. She wanted to experience a hug from Owen.

"I'll get the place-mats," Gregory said breaking into her thoughts. "I found Kris's Christmas napkins, too, on the bottom shelf in the pantry." He placed dark blue cloth mats on the table with a depiction of angels descending from a night sky over a stable surrounded by people and sheep.

"What is this?"

Owen turned around from the stove, glancing at the place-mats. "Bethlehem on Christmas night."

Angela looked back at Owen. "It was a cave."

Owen's eyebrow shot up. "Pardon?"

Angela realized she'd miss-stepped again. She had been one of those angels that night. But they wouldn't believe her.

Besides, revelations of this historical sort were not her assignment. "A painting I saw at Heavenly Acres depicted a cave."

Owen stirred the cocoa. "Yeah. I've heard that, too."

Gregory put out the plates. "So, what's in the bags, Angela?"

"Oh! Salad, bread, beets and vegetable pasta. Owen promised it was superior to the pasta at Heavenly Acres."

"It is a vegetarian meal, Dad. Good for all of us."

They all sat down to the table, Angela sat between both men, took their hands and bowed her head.

Owen and Gregory followed suit.

"Thank you," Angela said, picked up her fork and dug into the salad.

"Wait!" Owen protested. "That's it? That's your prayer?"

"Gratitude comes from the heart. Not the words," she beamed and munched on the delicious salad.

* * * * *

Angela sat on the edge of the bed looking out at the ebony sky. She had arrived on the earth planet on their winter solstice. It was the shortest day and the longest night of the year. It was the most positive night of the year. For six months, it would be the positive time of re-generation in the earth. The plants had gone dormant now, but their roots grew deeper into the earth. Seeds began drawing nourishment from the slow rest period until they would burst forth into the light. They would feed on the sun's energy and bring new life to their fruits and flowers.

All this life was created by love.

Love was the most magical mystery of all the universe, she thought. At that moment, Beau pranced into the room.

"Did you come to explain 'kiss' to me?" She asked.

"I will let you figure that out for yourself. Owen is changing his heart. He may not go back to Chicago."

"How would you know that?"

"I know a lot of things about humans."

Angela hugged Beau tightly and kissed his brow. "Dogs are wise."

A whirl of colored light filled the room. Angela jumped up and went to the window. At the top of the hill was the rainbow ball of light. It glowed faintly in the sky.

Beau came to stand beside her. He looked at the light as well. "What is it?" He asked telepathically.

She looked directly into the light. "No. Not yet," she said fiercely to the light. She turned around, went back to bed, and laid down.

Beau stared at the sky until the rainbow light vanished. Then he left to go to Gregory's room.

* * * * *

Angela was up early in the morning. Today was going to be an important day for her. And possibly for the entire family.

Before anyone else was up, except Beau, of course, she dressed and went to the kitchen where she turned on Gregory's radio that sat on the top of the refrigerator. She didn't like any of the sounds coming from the box. She remembered how she had programmed Owen's radio in his car to play peace-giving music. With a wave of her hand, she heard Debussy's Clair de lune and Suite bergamasque.

Holly and the children were coming over to teach her about cookies. She believed it was important for children to hear angelic music. It helped to raise their intelligence and make them happy. Music was a gift from heaven to the earth.

She was warming milk in a pan to make cocoa the way Owen made it, when Holly knocked on the back door. Angel opened the door for her.

"Good morning, Angela," Holly said handing Angela two cloth bags filled with grocery items, some of which Angela recognized. "The kids are bringing the powdered sugar, colors and sprinkles." She turned around. "Oh, here they are."

Mary walked in with a huge tin box. "This is every Christmas shape cutter we have. Mom's got Easter and Halloween cutters, too."

"I'll get the mixer out of the pantry," Joe said looking at Angela. "It is heavy. Then I have to help dad in the cow barn."

"Thank you," Holly said taking off her coat and putting the groceries on the table. She looked at Angela and said excitedly, "Are you ready to make cookies?"

"I am!"

Mary clapped her hands and jumped up and down. "This is almost as good as Christmas morning."

Joe plugged in the mixer and attached the beater for Mary. She took out a recipe card from a pretty binder book with a drawing of an angel in an apron holding a star shaped cookie in her hand. "See? Those are the best ones. Stars with lots of sprinkles," Mary said pointing to the picture for Angela to see.

Holly measured ingredients while Mary creamed the butter in the mixer. Holly and Mary demonstrated to Angela how they added the ingredients. First the sugar and creamed it, then the eggs and vanilla and then the mixture of the dry ingredients. Angela was very proud that by the end of the first batch, she had caught on quiet well.

Angela was given the task of rolling out the dough, while Mary cut the stars. Together they placed them on parchment paper lined cookie sheets. When the first tray was out of the oven, both Owen and Gregory had come to the kitchen and joined in the fun.

Holly made the frostings and Owen added the colors to several bowls. His favorite cookies were the Christmas trees.

Angela found the angel shaped cutter and asked Mary to cut out some for her. Holly started another batch of dough. Gregory put a tray full of Christmas tree shapes into the oven.

The kitchen was a whir of activity and lovely music when it was finally time to frost the cooled cookies.

Owen took a tree, slapped frosting on it, smeared it around and put a red cinnamon dot on the top of the tree. Then he picked up an angel and smeared it with white icing.

Angel watched him and asked, "What are you doing?" She wiped her hands on a towel as she looked at the cookie.

"Frosting the cookie."

"But that's an angel. She should have a beautiful face."

Owen looked at her askance. "And how would I do that?"

Angela took the cookie from him, dipped her finger in a glass of water and then into the pink icing and tried to finger paint the cookie. The colors ran together into a blur.

"This used to be easier," she complained.

Holly watched what Angela was doing and said, "Maybe you need paint brushes."

"I do?"

Gregory finished taking the last tray of angel cookies off the parchment and put them on the cooling racks. "Owen, I think I still have your mother's set of brushes. Over there in the desk drawer."

"Sure," Owen said and went to the kitchen desk and pulled out a pretty paint brush box. He handed it to Angela. "I remember her painting with these. She was such a good artist."

"She was, son," Gregory agreed.

Taking one of the brushes out, Angela felt the soft camel bristles. "How beautiful. I am honored to create with them."

Angela had never held an artist's brush but she had watched from high above as some of her "students" on other planets and time lines had painted with these utensils while they keyed into her creative ideas, visions, and guidance. She twirled the brush through her fingers, then wrapped her fingers around the smooth wooden handle. The balance was perfect.

She dipped the brush directly into the colors Owen was using, mixed them with water and a little white frosting to achieve the tone she wanted. She took her time, which was a new experience, but the face came together as she'd wished.

She took up another cookie.

Sam and Joe came in from the barn. Cold and hungry. Gregory put on another pot of coffee and made a new batch of cocoa. Joe leaned over the table where Angela was working. The angels, the trees, the stars, and the Santa's sleighs were beautiful, detailed, and ethereal.

"Cool."

Owen, who had been making grilled cheese sandwiches for everyone's lunch looked over at the cookies. "How did you do that?"

"I used to paint," Angela answered.

"Well, you're more than good." His eyes were filled with admiration.

Gregory picked up an angel she'd painted. "It's like looking at an oil painting. So realistic. You're quite talented."

Mary handed Angela a cookie. "Here's a Santa face. Do this one."

Joe said, "We need a picture to copy. Dad, gimme your cell phone. I'll find an app."

Sam opened the phone as he and Joe looked. "Those aren't right."

Angela smiled. "I know what Santa looks like."

Stunned and breathless, everyone in the room stared at her.

Owen was the first to speak. "Yeah? How's that?"

"I talked to him when he came over the first time," she said dipping her brush into the color and going to work.

Owen shared a concerned look with his father.

Owen couldn't let it go. He was enchanted by a enchantress. She was from another world. But what world? Another country? Or was she saying this because she thought she would please the kids? He guessed that Mary still believed in Santa Claus. Maybe that's all it was. Maybe.

"Came over where, Angela?" Owen gave in to his nagging paranoid-driven curiosity.

Just then Gregory sniffed the air. Holly was on the alert. She turned around, looked at the oven where brown smoke was coming out. "Oh no! Greg, you forgot the timer. Mitts! Please."

Owen took one step, grabbed the mitts from the top of the stove, opened the oven and pulled out the tray of very brown reindeer cookies. "Thank goodness they're reindeer."

"How come?" Mary asked.

"No need to frost them. They're perfect as they are."

Angela inspected the cookies. "Santa's reindeer have golden antlers."

Mary's eyes flew open. "Their antlers are gold?"

"And sparkling," Angela assured her. Angela looked up at Holly who smiled and mouthed:

"Thank you."

Owen looked at the array of cookies on the kitchen table, the desk, and the kitchen counters.

"Angela. You must have been some incredible artist before we met you. These look like Renaissance paintings. I've never seen anything like them. They're too beautiful to eat."

"That's right," Gregory said. "So, tonight let's say a prayer that Angela's cookies win the award."

Owen glanced at Angela. Her apron was covered with color and frosting. She had a splotch of frosting on her cheek. She couldn't have been any more adorable, he thought. He had to shake his head to clear it. "Um. That's right. The Christmas Cookie Exchange is tonight."

Sam had been cleaning up and Holly started packing up her supplies. "I need to get this family into the shower and dressed for the party."

"Party?" Angela asked not knowing what adventure they were taking her on now.

"What are you going to wear, Angela?" Holly asked.

"Wear?" Angel looked from Owen who looked stupefied to Gregory whose face lit up.

Gregory snapped his fingers. "I have just the thing."

* * * * *

Fourteen

Angela took a shower with a bar of rose smelling soap that Gregory said he'd found in one of Kris's lingerie drawers. Whatever that was. But the soap erased all the sticky frosting from her face, arms and even her hair. She'd never had to wash her hair. Again, this was a new experience. Owen showed her where the bottle of hair cleaning compound was. And then another compound she had to apply to "condition" her hair. Owen told her that her hair was so long and thick that it would take a great deal of both products to clean them properly and to avoid tangles. Whatever those were.

Fortunately, she was able to understand all their directions well enough that they didn't think her strange. She had learned by now to skirt the truth just a tiny bit so that she did not frighten them anymore about who she really was.

Nor would she ever disclose her true mission here.

She had come to learn that both Gregory and Owen had generous and loving hearts. Gregory had used his heart a great deal in his life, but he wasn't receiving love like he did when his wife was alive. She had also learned from her downloads from the Council, that this was a situation with many human beings. Love lost was often a death nell for far too many humans from what she had experienced. They spiraled down to lost hope and didn't know how to climb back to loving again. Gregory was trying.

He was blessed for that.

* * * * *

Owen wore a dark blue dress shirt, a navy and gold striped silk tie, black slacks, and his wing tips. He'd showered, shaved, and berated himself for missing his haircut appointment last week. He wanted to look his best tonight. Half of Black River would be there and the award for the best cookies was presented in his mother's honor. Tradition was that his father handed out the award every year. All eyes would be on Gregory, and possibly Owen.

On the bottom shelf in the back of the pantry, he found the kind of large plastic trays his mother used to use for the exchange. He'd just placed the first cookies on one of the trays when he glanced up and saw Angela standing in the doorway.

He was frozen. Speechless. He'd seen Julia wearing designer gowns and her mother's jewels, but she'd never stopped his heart beating like Angela.

He recognized the midnight blue belted cocktail dress with a wide full skirt that his mother had worn to his graduation party. It was simple. Sleeveless. V-neck. A gold buckle belt. No jewels, no sequins. Just a pair of black pumps. And cascades of Angela's glorious hair.

He would swear to the stars that he finally saw the shimmering, glimmering diamond light around her that Mary and Joe described.

"You are a vision."

She looked at him quizzically.

"I mean you look beautiful," he corrected. He didn't want her to think at this moment that he was criticizing her.

"And so are you." Her eyes beamed at him with an intensity that nearly made him rock back on his heels. How did she do that?

She looked down at the table. "What are you doing with the cookies?"

"I am putting the best ones on this tray---all the ones you decorated by the way. Then I'm covering them with this plastic wrap to preserve them so they don't dry out or get damaged. I plan to enter these in the auction tonight."

"Auction?"

"That's right. I bet someone will pay a pretty penny for these babies."

"I love pennies," she grinned. Then whispered to herself, "Especially the ones from heaven."

Owen placed sprigs of holly around the edges of the tray the way his mother had shown him. He finished covering the tray. "I'll take these out to the car. Do you mind putting the rest of the cookies on that tray and bring them to the car? I'll get it warmed up for us. Dad should be ready soon."

Owen left the kitchen. She placed the remaining cookies on another tray, then tucked the remaining holly pieces on the tray like how Owen had decorated his tray. Finally, she covered them with the wrap as Owen had done.

Gregory entered the kitchen dressed in a black suit and white shirt. He had an energetic glow.

"You are happy about this event," she said.

"And you are stunning in Kris's dress. I'm glad I kept it."

"Thank you for the gift of it. I will thank her as well." Angela stopped herself. She certainly did not want Gregory to know that she had seen Kris in Gregory's room at night when he slept. That information would lead to more questions from Owen. And he was getting too close to the truth as it was.

"You miss, Kris," Angela observed.

"Every day. I would give anything to hold her again."

"Heartfelt wishes come true especially at Christmas."

Gregory's intake of breath was audible. "She used to say that."

"Hmm. I am sure. It is a truism throughout the universe. She was a wise human."

Nodding, Gregory chuckled, "Certainly wiser than me." He glanced at his watch. "We better go. I'll get our coats."

"I'm to bring this tray."

"Ah. That's for the exchange. Sam and Holly are there setting up the booth."

"I'm happy to see them," she said, watching as Gregory went to the pegs in the hall and took down two parkas. One for her and one for himself. When he winced as he brought the parka to her, she did not react. She stood still as he held the parka for her. She put her arms into the sleeves. When she turned around, he was rubbing his arm.

Her eyes met his.

He could tell she knew what was happening.

She broke the silence. "This is a special night for Owen."

Angela slipped her arm through Gregory's as he asked, "Why do you say that?"

"Because he's beginning to see the light."

"That'll be the day," Gregory chuckled as they went out the front door.

* * * * *

The shoveled pave stone walkway up to the Black River Town Center Barn was lined with tall Bradford Pear trees each strung with a thousand crystal lights. Interspersed with the live trees were shorter evergreen Christmas trees in tin buckets lit with multi-colored lights and wooden ornaments in the shape of sleds, gingerbread men, and mittens.

Hanging on the red painted front doors of the barn were two enormous green wreaths. A thick garland of greens, red ribbons and multicolored lights swept across the entire front of the barn. Music from a country western band filled the air each time the doors were opened.

"It's beautiful," Angela said, carrying her cookie tray as they walked up.

"Those wreaths don't hold a candle to yours you made for us," Owen said as Gregory opened the door.

"Ditto that, son."

Holding the cookie tray in his right hand, Owen placed his left hand on the small of Angela's back. For the second time, he was shocked at his reaction. This time, he felt undeniably protective toward Angela. Her long hair felt like silk against his bare hand, as a tingle of goosebumps raced up his arm. He didn't remove his hand. He wanted to keep it there. All night.

She didn't flinch or shake off his gesture as sometimes Julia did. Well, many times. Okay, Owen, he confessed to himself. Most of the time.

"I have to take these cookies to the judges' table," Owen said turning to Gregory. "You'll help Angela with her coat?"

"Sure will, son," Gregory replied taking off his parka.

Owen's eyes widened. "You wore your tux?"

Gregory beamed. "Still fits. That's a Christmas miracle," he laughed.

Owen took the tray to the judges' table and scoped out the competition. He rubbed his hands together. "Cake walk," he said and the looked into the face of Sally Wainright.

He gulped. Of all the judges they could possibly have chosen this year, Sally was the most discerning. And the toughest. A gourmet cook in her own right, she'd written two cookbooks, one of which made the Chicago Tribune's Bestseller list. She had her own streaming cooking show. And she lectured throughout the mid-west. Sally was a legend. She was still a Black River resident and had been a friend of his mother.

This was not a good sign.

Owen knew that after the auction itself, Sally would taste a pre-selected cookie from each tray in the auction. It was her decision who would win the Best Cookie Award that night. His father wore his tux which also told Owen that Gregory expected Angela's cookies, their cookies, to win the Black River Cookie Exchange Award. No wonder his dad looked so energized tonight. He had high hopes. Very high hopes.

If their cookies didn't win, Gregory would be crestfallen. Now Owen felt guilty for setting up his dad, Angela, Holly, Sam, and the kids for what he had believed was a shoe-in win.

Angela's cookies were stunning, but did they taste good? They'd all mixed, baked and frosted together. Who knew which one Sally would taste? He hoped he hadn't mistakenly put a burnt reindeer on the tray.

"Hello, Sally," Owen beamed as he walked up to Sally. She was impeccably dressed and though she was nearly eighty, she looked twenty-five years younger. Sally was wealthy now. He guessed she could afford the best plastic surgeon in Chicago.

"Owen, you handsome devil. So, you finally came home for Christmas," she leveled a steely blue eye on him.

"I did."

"I heard about Greg. How is he?" She glanced across the full expanse, past the people dancing and the band at the far end of the barn.

"Doing great," Owen replied.

She pointed to his tray but didn't look at them. "Those are yours?"

"It was a group effort, you could say."

"Hmm. Well, have a good evening." She wiggled her fingers at him and walked over to speak to another couple placing their entry cookie tray.

Owen whisked off his overcoat and took a deep breath as he crossed the barn in search of Angela and his dad. He hung his coat in the cloak room. Adjusting his suit jacket sleeves as he walked out of the cloak room, he scanned the barn.

From the rafters hung more lights than Julia had strung at the Yacht club. Garlands and ribbons were draped over every doorway and window. Lighted Christmas trees lined the walls making Owen wonder if there were any more trees left standing in Black River.

The Pine Tree Christmas farm did a bang-up business this year, he mused. Maybe he should visit them. Perhaps they would need an estate planner.

Circling the perimeter were booths and tables where every kind of traditional Christmas cookie, Stollen, fruit cake, homemade caramels and chocolates, jams, jellies and other baked goods were sold.

The music was lively and fun and there was a stage set up next to the band. Next to it was as fifteen-foot tree that was decorated with candy canes, lollipops, garlands of mints and cookies hung by yarn. Large gingerbread men danced along strings of cranberries and popcorn. This was the Sugarplum tree that his mother had established. It, too, was auctioned off and the proceeds went to the Black River Town Center.

To his left was a Santa seated in a velvet chair with a toddler on his lap. A photographer snapped a photo. The mother of the child hoisted the little boy into her arms and thanked Santa.

Finally, Owen spied Angela and his father who was being stopped by several of his friends. They greeted each other with guffaws and pats on the back. He was struck by how genuine their smiles were. Gregory took the time to introduce Angela to his friends.

I wonder how he's doing that? Angela was what? A girl who appeared on their hilltop?

Owen picked up his pace as Angela followed Gregory to the booth marked "Exchange Cookies." The booth was fashioned out of plywood to look like an old English bakery with a red and white striped canvas awning overhead. Holly and Sam stood behind the table.

Owen stood next to Angela as she handed the tray to Holly.

Sam was beaming. "I've been bragging on your cookies all evening, Angela."

"Thank you, Sam. May I ask? What do you exchange for the cookies?"

"Money," Sam laughed.

Owen leaned closer to Angela and put his hand on her arm. "It's a fund-raiser." He swallowed a lump in his throat. His hand felt inordinately good on her arm.

She looked up at him. "I hope they help."

Holly moved a tray to make room for Angela's addition. "Sam thinks this will be our best auction ever."

"I do," Sam said. "Last year we raised over two thousand dollars."

Owen whistled. "For cookies?"

"Not just for the cookies, Owen. We are sponsoring a mentor program for special needs kids in Black River."

"What do you teach them?" Angela was curious.

"Everything from reading to music to---"

"Art?" She interrupted.

Sam shook his head. "I wish. We sure would if we had a teacher." His expression brightened. "Say, Angela would you consider teaching the kids? I mean it's a donation of your time. We can't pay much."

Holly interrupted. "That's why the auction is necessary. If we raise enough money, we can afford a teacher."

"Right," Sam agreed.

"Teaching would be different here," Angela said, thinking of the difficulty of matching frequencies to most humans. Teaching assignments in the celestial realm were positions of highly evolved energy beings. She was a muse. But was she a teacher?

Peering at her, Owen was sincere when he said, "You'd be good at it."

"Do you think so?"

"I do." *And you'd have to move here. Live here.*

The band ended the lively country song and began a melodic Christmas song. A soloist stepped to the microphone and sang the nostalgic lyrics.

Owen slid his hand down and laced his fingers through Angela's. "Dance with me."

"Dance? I do not know---"

Smiling broadly, he pulled her toward the dance floor. "I'll show you. Just hold onto me."

* * * * *

Fifteen

They wove their way through the shoppers and the crowd to the dance floor. Owen lifted Angela's left arm and put it on his shoulder. He placed her right hand in his and laid them both over his heart.

Angela tried to follow his steps. It was hard enough balancing on legs to walk. Now she was hoping he didn't knock her over with this shuffling of his feet. But his shoulders and arms were strong and held her each time she faltered.

This warmth between them when their bodies were this close caused a myriad of sensations in her. Calculating the extent of them was an exercise in focus. And that was the problem.

When Owen placed his cheek next to hers, she could hear his breath and feel the pulse of his heart alongside his throat. Melding together was a new experience. She'd been an inspiration to humans and other races throughout the galaxy but she'd never melded with another consciousness and certainly not in this manner that encompassed the area from the top of her head to the bottom of her feet.

As the music swelled, she noticed that Owen would pull her closer. His thigh would sometimes rub against hers. He pressed her hand tighter to his chest.

This was a time when she wished she was telepathic with him because she would like to know if he was experiencing any of the sensations that she did. Perhaps this was something that happened to angels when they came to earth. Not having lived in a human body, she didn't understand the prickles that covered her arms when his breath cascaded down her neck.

When he whispered some of the words of the song in her ear, she had the sensation of leaving this body. She floated for a moment, especially when she closed her eyes. The only way she could keep her balance was to open her eyes and focus on a single point.

That strategy did not work, either, as Owen spun her around in a circle, still clutching her next to him. "I'm off balance," she said as she stumbled.

"Okay. I'll take it easy on you."

Keeping her eyes open was key, she realized. In addition, she was able to appreciate the details the artists created making this barn merry.

"All these decorations are so beautiful. Special."

"They are. Back when my mom created the Cookie Exchange night, none of the families had much money for fancy decorations. We all made ornaments from popsicle sticks, string, pine cones, and glitter. We hung cookies and candy canes on the tree."

"I would like to see those."

"Dad says they are all gone. Rotted. Tomorrow is Christmas Eve and that is when we decorated the tree."

"That's why there are only lights on it now?"

"Yes, it's waiting for Christmas," he said.

"What does that mean to you, Owen?"

"It used to mean the usual. Santa. Presents," he smiled.

"And now?"

"I'd forgotten…until a few moments ago."

"What happened?"

"I put my arms around you," he said seriously. His eyes filled with wonder. They touched Angela's heart.

"Oh," she said and laid her head on his shoulder.

Suddenly, the song ended and the people around them clapped their hands together.

"I've always loved that song," Owen said as he took her arm from his shoulder, but held onto her hand. His eyes probed her face and fell to her mouth. She didn't know what he was thinking, as hard as she tried to reach his subconscious.

"What was the song?"

"Blue Christmas."

He lifted her hand and pressed her palm to his lips. "I've had too many blue Christmases."

She stared at him as he slowly pulled away from her palm. Every thought in her head jumbled. Her teeth vibrated and a strong pulse shot through her third eye. Blood surged through her temples and her legs went numb. She slumped against him. "Oh!"

He held her upright and hugged her to his chest.

"Are you okay?"

"I like your...hugs."

"And the dancing? With me?"

She sensed anxiety ripple through him as his hand trembled slightly. The thought that her answer meant a great deal to him flitted through her head. "I liked it."

"A little or a lot?"

"Very much."

"Before the night is over, will you dance with me again?"

"Yes."

Their eyes were locked on each other as Sam bounded onto the stage, and took the microphone from the soloist. "Good evening, everyone and Merry Christmas!"

Owen pulled his eyes from Angela and she felt the rift. Separation, she thought as the warmth they had shared faded.

"Let's hear it for the Black River Band," Sam said applauding loudly into the microphone. The dancers and shoppers gathered around the stage. Gregory walked over to stand next to Angela and Owen.

Sam continued. "It's time for the cookie auction. My lovely wife, Holly will bring up the first item for auction. Remember, folks, the money goes to support the Black River Children's Mentor Program."

Holly walked onto the stage with a silver tray of gingerbread men.

Three well-dressed men in suits and ties worked their way from the back of the room to the front near Gregory.

Gregory tapped Owen on the shoulder. "Here they come."

"Who?" Owen asked looking around.

"Ed Withers has gained a few pounds and some years since you were home last. And a good deal of cash. Next to him wearing the cowboy boots with his fancy Italian suit is Wilburn Garrick. I just went to his seventieth bash. He's made a killing with his granary company. They vie with each other every year over the cookies. It's all ego, if you ask me. But it's the newcomer, Jerry West over there. Whipper snapper. Only fifty who works from home. Some kinda app designer Sam says. He comes here to outbid everybody."

"This is fun," Owen chuckled.

"Better than horse racing." This," Gregory pointed to Sam. "...will make my year."

Owen gulped.

"Like last year," Sam began. "We have Anna Marks' annual Gingerbread men. We all know how tasty these guys are. Who'll give me fifty dollars for two dozen of these fellas?"

Owen raised his hand, but Ed Withers beat him to it by shouting out, "Fifty dollars!"

"Do I hear one hundred?" Sam shouted into the microphone while scanning the crowd.

"One hundred," Wilburn Garrick offered.

"Two hundred." Bid Ed Withers.

Sam looked back to Wilburn who shook his head. "Sold! To Ed Withers for two hundred."

The crowd roared and applauded.

Holly walked onto the stage with a straw cornucopia filled with several kinds of cookies. "This fantastic display was gifted by Silvia West. Who'll give me a hundred dollars for this beauty?"

"One hundred," Wilburn bid.

Jerry West shouted, "Aw c'mon. It cost more than that. Three hundred for my wife's cherished recipes."

Ed Withers smiled triumphantly. "Four hundred." Clearly, he thought he had won.

Jerry West pursed his lips. "Five hundred."

Wilburn took a step forward, thumbs stuck in his belt. "Seven hundred if she throws in the secret recipes."

Sylvia West, a pretty fifty-year old chestnut-haired woman, in a Christmas dress and high healed leather boots shouldered her way to the front of the crowd. "Never!"

Ed Withers guffawed and shouted even louder. "Eight hundred. That Missy has spunk!"

Sam exclaimed, "Going once, twice. Sold! To Ed Withers. No recipes included."

Holly then brought up the tray of Angela's painted portrait cookies. Carefully, she walked to the edge of the stage to show off the artistry.

Sam's voice was prideful as he said, "Few of you know Gregory and Owen Michael's Christmas visitor, Angela, but Holly and I have gotten to know her pretty well. She's as sweet as sugar and painted these exceptional cookies for our auction."

Owen smiled at Angela and put his arm around her shoulder as the people turned to gaze at Owen and nod their approval.

Sam announced, "Do I hear a bid for one hundred?"

From the back of the room a patron shouted, "One hundred."

"Two fifty," another man's voice yelled.

"Five hundred," Ed Withers bid after looking closely at the tray Holly was showing to him.

Jerry West whose wife, Sylvia was tugging on his coat sleeve, yelled out, "One thousand, Sam."

Several in the crowd gasped.

The man in the back of the barn shouted, "Twelve hundred."

Sylvia West stepped up to the edge of the stage, motioned to Sam to give her the microphone. "Fifteen hundred dollars," she said fiercely and handed the microphone back to Sam.

Sam searched the crowd. No more bids came forth. "Going. Going. Sold! Sylvia West."

The applause was deafening. Angela had to put her hands over her ears, but when she did, Owen swept her up in his arms and whirled her around. She wasn't quite sure what was happening but she keyed into the strong frequency in the room that she knew for a fact that it could lift the building from the earth.

Mary and Joe rushed up to Angela to hug her. Greg put his punch cup down and applauded with the audience.

Suddenly, he winced. He held his left arm.

At the onset of Gregory's pain, Angela looked over the children's heads and watched Gregory. She was not allowed to interfere. This was expected.

Sam quieted the crowd down. "Folks, this is a magical night. We have just made history. As our highest ever winning bid for the cookie exchange auction we all thank you, Angela."

She didn't know what to say. She turned to Owen.

He smiled. "Just say thank you."

"Blessings."

Sam was joined on stage by Sally Wainright and Gregory who held a brass Christmas tree shaped plaque for the Christmas Cookie Exchange Award. "And now, ladies and gentlemen, the moment we've all been waiting for. The presentation of our esteemed award. Sally Wainright has tasted all the cookies submitted to the judging. And she's picked the winner."

Sam handed Sally the microphone. "To keep the judging fair, I asked my associates to move the trays around and for them to number each tray so that I could be totally impartial. They selected one cookie from each tray with its coinciding number."

As the anticipation elevated, Sally continued. "Again, I will say some of the best pastries in Wisconsin come from Black River. Perhaps it is our grass-fed cow's milk and butter. Perhaps is the care of the bakers. All the entries were exceptional this year. I doubt I could do better myself."

She continued. "However, these sugar cookies were supreme. I would tell the baker, never to share this recipe." She read from a green colored piece of paper. "This was tray number seven. It belongs to Owen Michaels."

Gregory was the first to shout, "Yesss!" He lifted the award over his head for everyone to see.

Angela felt Owen's arms encircle her waist from behind. "You won, Angela. Go up there and get your award."

"But we all did it. I do not know how to make cookies."

"You do now." He said taking her hand.

Angela spun around to Mary and Joe. "Come with me. You helped."

"Are you sure?" They asked in unison.

"I am."

Owen pulled Angela, who held Mary's hand and was followed by Joe. They all walked up the steps to the stage. Gregory was overjoyed to hand the award to Angela. She quickly gave the award to the children.

Sam held the microphone to Angela's mouth.

Her look was quizzical.

Owen leaned over. "You have to say something to the people."

Angel looked at over a hundred happy, excited faces. She felt their admiration and their joy. These were Gregory's friends and acquaintances all through his life. They had invested their hearts in him. And he in they. They were community.

That was a concept she understood.

"We did it together. Sam, Holly, Mary, Joe, Owen, Gregory, and me. This joy is best because we share it with you."

A hush fell over the crowd. Then they burst into cheers and applause.

Sam took the microphone again and quieted the crowd. "That just about wraps up our evening. So, to end the night we will all sing our annual Christmas Carol."

The lights in the rafters were extinguished leaving only the lights on the trees on the main floor.

To Angela the barn and the people in it appeared even more magical. Owen leaned close and whispered, "You don't dance but do you sing?"

"I sing," she replied with a soft smile.

"Good."

The band assembled behind them on the stage as Sam announced, "We always sing the Hallelujah Chorus."

Owen held Angela's hand and squeezed it. "Do you know this song?"

"My favorite."

The band played the overture as the group on the floor began singing. Angela was slow to start, but as their voices blended, she closed her eyes remembering how she sang with the other angels this most heavenly music.

Angela did not realize that as the song continued, her voice rose higher and higher. She felt the vibration of the music in her human throat and it resonated throughout her body. She was uplifted. She was in that other world.

Owen looked at Angela as did Gregory, Holly, and the kids. Sam slid behind Angela and held the microphone just below her shoulders so as not to miss a single extraordinary note. A boy in the back of the barn opened the barn doors to allow the music to waft outside.

Owen glanced at Sam who was as dumbfounded as he. He'd never heard a voice like Angela's. He was awestricken.

The song ended.

Silence hung in the barn as the last vestiges of Angela's melodic timbres floated out to the surrounding countryside.

The hush of awe and wonder fell over the crowd. Something astonishing had just happened.

Sylvia West whispered to her husband, "As choral director for the high school and having been in music all my life, I'm telling you that Angela, whoever she is, has a voice that is higher than normal human range. And she held her notes longer than is humanly possible."

"Really?"

"Where did Gregory say she's from?"

"He didn't," Jerry replied.

Sylvia watched as the Michael's group left the stage. "Well, wherever it is, it must be magical.

*****

Sixteen

The advantage that angels have when they come to earth is that they are not required to sleep. During that time in the dark night, Angela connected with informative angels and spirits in several different dimensions of the celestial realm.

This night, Angela needed help from Owen's mother, Kris.

After all, angels and spirits worked together in several dimensions. Angela remembered that Kris watched over Gregory when he slept. She was close to him during the day as well, but at night, Gregory, like most humans who are open to the spiritual realms and beliefs, often received Kris's love and messages in his dreams.

By the act of thinking about Kris, then summoning the spirit to her, Owen's mother appeared in the room. Angela's first joy was that she and Kris could transmit thoughts telepathically. It took less energy. Because they were both not "of the earth plane" there was no construed communication as there was between Angela and Owen.

"Kris," Angela relayed telepathically. "I am grateful for your help."

"You help my son."

"It's a struggle."

"I am aware. He was not this blocked when he was young."

"Your death severed the silver cords of mother and son bonds. He has not recovered."

"I'm told not to feel guilty about this," Kris relayed.

"Never. Guilt in any dimension is a waste of spirit. This is Owen's lesson in life to learn," Angela added.

"Must it be done quite so painfully?"

"Humans appear to learn things the hard way," Angela replied telepathically.

"What you are doing for him now, will bring joy."

"That is my intention," Angela answered. "Time to work."

Kris was able to tell Angela exactly where she would find the box of the old Christmas ornaments. She also needed instructions how Kris constructed these special ornaments and where she would find the tools and the objects that Owen referred to as popsicle sticks, glitter, glue, and cotton.

Just after midnight when Owen had turned off his computer and Gregory was asleep, Angela went out the kitchen door. She was just about to close the door when Beau came padding into the kitchen.

"Where are you going?" Beau asked telepathically.

"Hunting," she said holding up a brown paper bag.

"That's not how I hunt," Beau said.

She walked toward the hill with the pines and evergreens. "I'll ask the trees but I think they will be happy to share their pinecones."

Beau followed her. "Pinecones. Not as much fun as squirrels. They like the chase."

"You can play with your friends later. I have work to do."

Angela went to a copse of pine trees and was about to ask permission for their pinecones, when she noticed the snow was dotted with dozens of cones. "You see? The trees knew I was coming. Thank you for these beautiful gifts," she said.

It didn't take long for Angela to fill her bag. She did not like the sticky pine goo that Beau told her was pine sap. It was all over her hands. They went back to the house where she scrubbed her hands with soap and a scratchy sponge, she had watched Owen use to clean the cocoa pot.

Once her hands were smooth again, she went to the pantry and in the far back corner she found a brown cardboard box filled with the "craft" tools Kris told her she had used. Kris explained she would need tweezers which she pinched together to pick up items, to fill the pinecones with cotton balls.

She was to glue the popsicle sticks together in the shape of stars and then twist blue yarn from stick to stick to create the look Owen was expecting. She glued yarn to the heads of gingerbread men cookies. She found the box of brand-new candy canes that Gregory had bought and unwrapped them.

She took the cranberries out of the refrigerator and found a bag of popped corn also in the large pantry. She remembered seeing the string of red and white units on the trees at the Black River Barn that night. It was not difficult to copy them.

She turned on the tree lights and sighed at the loveliness. Hanging the ornaments on the tree was a most delightful task, she discovered. It was a wonder human beings didn't have Christmas trees all year.

She found a very old creche in a box in the hall closet. Just where Kris told her it was. She put the figurines under the tree and sighed again. That had been a beautiful night.

Angela did not realize the sun had risen; she was so busy working on the ornaments for the tree. She had just finished glittering a pine cone when Owen walked into the kitchen. His hair was rumpled. He wore a faded tee shirt and a pair of baggy pants on which were emblazed in white letters, "Santa, I can explain" down both legs.

She could not help comparing this Owen to the one who was dressed in a suit and determined to be rid of her.

"Mornin'," he yawned. "How long have you been up?"

"Oh, I don't sleep," she blurted and then realized she had made a mistake.

"Ever?"

"I mean, not when there is much to do."

He gazed at the mess on the table. Newspapers, brown paper bags of pine cones. Glitter and glue. Yarn. Ribbons. "What, may I ask are you doing?"

"It's Christmas Eve."

"I know that but this…"

"Go into the living room," she suggested and rose from her chair.

He rubbed his eyes as he walked down the hall. "What in the world?"

"You are displeased," she observed deflated.

"No. The opposite. I love it," he walked over to the tree and touched the new ornaments Angela had made.

"I found the ones your mother made with you," she said waving her hand over a group of older homemade ornaments she'd placed on the coffee table. "I left them for you to hang."

Gregory walked into the room and stopped abruptly, looking agape, eyes filled with wonder at the tree. "Who's the elf?"

"That would be Angela," Owen said, holding a popsicle and yarn star in his hand.

"Why," Gregory began going over to the tree, his eyes filled with awe. "It's just like Kris would have done. She always decorated the tree while I was napping. I'd wake up and voila!

There was this beautiful, magical tree. You know what she would always say to me?"

"No, Dad. What?"

"Magic is something we make." He beamed at Owen and then at Angela. "Thank you, Angela."

Gregory bent over the array of ornaments on the coffee table. "Hmph. I swear I threw these out years ago. They were rotted."

Angela's knowing smile crooked the corners of her mouth. "They are not."

"Musta missed a box, huh, Dad?"

Beau padded into the room and went straight to Angela, rubbed his head against her leg. She petted him. He looked up at her. "My lips are sealed," Beau sent her the thought.

"They wouldn't hear you anyway."

"Yeah, humans."

Owen went straight to work hanging the old ornaments on the tree.

As he did, Gregory looked over to the sofa and clear as day, he saw Kris sitting on the sofa in her favorite bell-bottom jeans, smiling at him.

"I love you," Kris sent the thought to Gregory.

As Kris's words struck him, Gregory felt the room around him evaporate into a white mist. In this dreamworld, there was only Kris and himself. She looked real. Not transparent any more. For a split second he thought he might be allowed to touch her hand. To hold her.

As the thought filtered through his consciousness, the mist began to fade. Kris turned transparent again. "Is there a reason why you're here so much this Christmas?"

The words were no more out of his mouth, when he felt like he'd been dropped into the earth plane. He was back. The living room was back. He saw Angela, not Kris. He heard Owen's voice. "Did you say something, Dad?"

"No," Gregory's voice cracked missing Kris, even in spirit.

"Okay." Owen put another glitter covered pinecone on the tree. There wasn't much glitter left, but it was the old multi-colored glitter of red, green, gold and silver he remembered. At that moment, he sniffed the air. "I know this tree smells like pine and citrus, but does anybody else smell lavender?"

"I smell roses," Gregory replied picking up a candy cane shaped ornament made of red and white faded pipe cleaners.

"That would be Angela," Owen smiled.

She smiled back. "The soap---is rose." She was always covering up her mistakes. One little slip and she would learn about it from The Other Side.

Gregory stopped mid-motion. "Lavender? Kris sometimes wore lavender body splash."

Angela settled her eyes on the sofa where Kris had been sitting. She was still there, but this time, did Gregory see her?

Angela looked at Gregory. Rubbing his eyes, he stared at the sofa. He looked at Angela and from the blank look on his face, Angela knew that he no longer saw Kris.

Gregory rubbed his forehead as if his finger pressure would help collect his thoughts.

"Gimme another star, please Angela," Owen asked still focused on his job at hand. "And there's a bare spot here perfect for a big gingerbread man. That was genius to put these yarn hangers on your cookies, Angela."

She was aware that Owen was oblivious to the exchange she and Gregory had experienced with Kris.

"We haven't had any breakfast," Gregory said. "I'll take orders."

"Cocoa, please for me," Angela's smile filled her face.

"Do you ever want anything else?" Owen asked.

She thought for a minute. "A reindeer cookie."

Owen burst out laughing. "I can't say that there's a better breakfast for Christmas Eve."

Gregory frowned. "What would your mother say? I'll scramble some eggs to go with those cookies."

"I'll take three," Owen said. "I'm starved. This is mentally taxing---decorating."

"I thought it was fun," Angela said handing him another ornament.

"Yeah, too much fun, really. You're right. And as soon as I finish, I have work to do. And---I should pack."

Gregory stopped in the hallway and marched back to the living room. "I heard that. You're packing? It's Christmas Eve."

"Yes. And that means I have to get back to Julia."

Angela's eyes flew to Gregory. He was crestfallen.

"Owen's right. Fun's over. Time for work," Gregory bit off the words.

"Work?" Angela asked.

"Sam just drove up. I should help with the calves."

Angela rose. "I'll help."

She went to Gregory and took his arm.

"Thank you, Angela,"

Neither of them said a word to Owen.

* * * * *

Seventeen

On the Michael's farm near the milking parlor was a line of calf hutches which were individual little houses, Gregory explained to Angela. "This is where the newborns are brought after birth. As you see, they have a very clean little white plastic house to live in. Joe and Mary clean out their hutch every day and place new hay, water, and feed."

"That fence?"

"That's their play area, I call it. Mainly, it's to give them room to grow."

They continued walking down the snowy lane between the row of hutches. Angela asked a myriad of question.

Gregory, however, was fascinated by the number of rabbits, squirrels and chipmunks that scampered out from under the pines and evergreens and followed them.

At the house, Owen folded a sweater to pack. When he passed by the window, he glanced out and noticed Angela and his father walking. What interested him most was the growing animal menagerie marching behind them. Two cardinals flew overhead, circled, and came back around. "Air patrol?"

The cardinals were joined by two more. All four hovered over Angela for a long moment. Owen half-expected them to land on her shoulder for a ride.

"So now she's the pied piper?"

Even the woodland animals feel her magnetism.

* * * * *

When Angela and Gregory walked up to the milking parlor, Holly was working with Mary to fill fresh water into the water troughs. Joe was feeding the cows. One of the calves stood next to its mother. Angela could not resist stroking the baby calf's head. "He's so sweet," she cooed.

"This one is only a week old. We decided to keep him in here where it is very warm," Holly said. "I'm convinced we'll have another new baby by tomorrow."

"Tomorrow?" Gregory hooted. "A Christmas baby. I hope it's a girl."

"Is that better?" Angela asked.

"For us, yes. The mother's give milk. The males we sell to Tom Hickey down the road."

Angela didn't want to stop stroking the calf. She made eye contact with him. What a sweet soul he has," she said. "So precious."

Mary came over and petted the calf as well. "I love him, too."

Holly asked, "Greg. Where's Owen? I thought he'd be with you."

Mary smiled broadly. "Me, too. I hope when I grow up, I can dance like you and Owen did last night."

Holly's eyes filled with shock. "Mary!"

"I thought they were---" she smoothed her hand over the calf's head, "…you know, romantic."

"Mary, sweetheart. Why don't you get that fresh grain for me?"

Mary's shoulders slumped. "Okaaaay." She tromped off reluctantly.

Holly moved closer to Angela. "I apologize for Mary. She can be precocious."

"I don't know what that is, but she's wonderful."

"I can tell by the look on your face that Owen is leaving."

Her hand flew to her cheek. "You can see that?"

"You're pretty transparent."

"I am?" Stunned, Angela quickly looked at her legs to check if she was disappearing. "I don't mean to be."

"That's a compliment."

"Oh." Angela was glad she knew that a 'compliment' was a good thing.

While Gregory worked with Joe, Holly walked over to the parlor door which was slightly ajar. She looked to the farm house and saw Owen watching them through his window.

She turned back to Angela. "I was hoping he would stick around. For his dad."

Angela went to the door and looked out. Owen looked straight at her. She gazed back at him. "I had faith that he would do it for himself."

"You did?"

"Owen is a good man. A very good man. But he forgot some things."

Holly clucked her tongue and said, "I'll say."

* * * * *

Owen came away from the window, his suitcase half packed. He took out the sweater he'd just folded and pulled it over his head. He went to the hall hooks, grabbed one of his dad's work jackets. He found a pair of work gloves in the pocket. At the back kitchen door were "slop boots" that were used when working in the barn and hutches. He put the boots on thinking: *one glance from Angela and I'm as hypnotized as those rabbits and birds. If she had cast a spell on me, I couldn't be more bewitched.*

Maybe that's what she was. Enchantress. Yes. All the way. But no, she was different. He'd had crushes before. Infatuations. But Angela drew him because of her goodness. She didn't make sense half the time, but she spoke her heart. That he did believe.

And I can't stay away from her more than a few minutes.

He walked out of the frosty air and into the milking parlor. He closed the door. "Mornin' Holly. "

"Owen," Holly replied turning off the water hose.

Angela turned and when their eyes met and she smiled at him, he felt jittery and as clumsy as a teenager.

"I'm learning about the calves," Angela said.

"That used to be my job when I was Mary's age."

"You liked it?" she asked.

"No." He smiled. "I loved it." He glanced behind him. "I was thinking, before I leave, I should show you some of my favorite places around the farm."

"Thank you," she replied and as she walked to him, she took his hand in hers. "You should hold my hand. Before I go away."

"You mean before I go away," he corrected. "I'm the one who's leaving."

Owen took Angela to the very large cow barn. This was a wide expanse, completely covered with fresh hay. The cows slept on the floor. Some slept curled around each other, especially the mothers and the calves.

"What a magnificent sight," Angela gasped.

"This is my favorite place."

As they walked through the barn, one of the calves stood up, went to Angela, and put his head under her palm.

"She wants a pet."

"She wants a blessing. Every time I touch them, I am sending them love."

He watched her. Watched the calf who was luxuriating in her every touch. "Yes. I believe you are."

Another calf ambled over for his few minutes with Angela.

Owen smiled as yet another calf vied for her attention. "They like you."

"I like them very much. They are such giving souls, aren't they?"

He tilted his head. "They're animals."

One of the mother cows lifted her head and mooed at Owen. Angela laughed.

"Owen. They give their milk. Even their lives to feed humans. Generous."

He blew out a breath that inflated his cheeks. "Guess that puts me in my place. You sure view the world from a different perspective, don't you?"

"I thought there was only one."

"And that is?"

"Love."

"Yes. Well..." She was doing it again. Drawing him in and if he knew what that was exactly, he might be all in, but she was a mystery. Too much of a mystery. He swallowed and cleared this throat. "Well, that area over there has to be mucked I heard Sam say yesterday. It's ready for fresh hay."

He went to the wall and took a pitch fork from a peg. He began cleaning away the old hay. "When the other cows come back from the milking parlor, they'll appreciate this."

Angela went past one of the bales of hay on her way to get a pair of large sheers to cut the binding, when she noticed three white feathers on top of the hay bale. She picked them up.

"Owen! Look! Three feathers stuck together!"

Owen joined her and inspected the feathers. "That's odd."

"No."

"It's the dead of winter, Angela. I haven't seen bird feathers in a long, long time. These are not Blue Jay or Cardinal feathers."

"You should pay attention."

"And you are doing that?" He didn't know exactly where she was going with this---always a problem with Angela---but he didn't like the way she appeared to be chastising him.

"Yes, Owen. Feathers are a sign."

"Oh, here we go."

"You don't believe?"

"What? That there's something magical going on? No. Quite frankly, I don't."

"I'm sorry." Angel walked off.

"You're angry with me?"

"No. Worse. Disappointed."

Owen rushed after her, took her arm and pulled her to his chest. Without thinking, he put his hand on her nape, and kissed her. She was pliant, willing and the longer he held her, the more responsive she became, though she stood stock still. There was no passion. No anger. No need or ego.

There was love. And it knocked him from one end of the universe to the other.

He was doing the kissing, exerting himself, but she had him.

He didn't know what to do, other than to never let this end. But it had to end.

Reluctantly, he left her lips. Her eyes were closed. He was still wafting through another place and time.

"What---was that?" she whispered as she opened her blue eyes and probed his face with more innocence than he'd ever seen.

"Yours was the most amazing kiss of my life."

"My only kiss."

"Not really?"

She nodded.

"Truly? Wow."

"But not yours."

Still gazing into her eyes he wished he was sixteen and she was his first kiss. It felt like his first. "No. Not my first. Angela, I don't know anything about you. Where you're from and frankly, everything about you is a mystery. But this is, er, unexpected and confusing."

"I felt it was sweet."

Owen couldn't wait to go back to that space where she'd taken him. He pulled her close again and was about to kiss her again, when Joe burst through the huge barn door.

"Owen! Angela! Dad says come quick! The calf is coming."

"A baby born," Angela gushed.

"A cow anyway," Owen grumbled.

"A new experience," Angela replied excitedly.

"I guess it would be for you. I think---" he paused. "Well, let's hurry." He grabbed Angela's hand and they took off running after Joe.

* * * *

Eighteen

The baby calf stumbled on his newborn legs.

Angela's thought, "I know exactly this experience, little one," blurted out of her mouth. It had been only days ago that she had tumbled to earth and had to navigate her movements on a pair of human legs. But this baby calf would grow to maturity on earth. She would not.

"That sight never gets old." The pride in Gregory's voice drew smiles and nods of agreement.

Sam, who had delivered the calf, began cleaning up the area with Holly's help. Joe took photos on his dad's cell phone.

"Can I print these out and take to school for my friends to see?" Joe asked.

"Me, too?" Mary asked.

"Oh, Joe," Holly laughed. "Not only did you take a photo last week of the other calf, but half those kids live on farms and have their own calves they brag about."

Shoving the cell phone in his back jeans' pocket. "But our calf is the best looking."

Gregory howled and slapped Joe on the back. "Spoken like a true dairy farmer." Gregory hugged him.

Owen was shocked at the streak of jealousy that shot up his spine. I'm jealous of my dad hugging young Joe? Owen had only just met Sam, Holly, and the family. Frankly, he didn't even know they lived next door and he had not paid attention when his dad had mentioned them in phone calls. Owen hadn't paid attention to much about his dad except for how poorly the farm was doing and what could be done to increase revenue streams. If he'd been more cognizant of the farm and it's day to day operation, then he might have a reason, slight as it was, to be jealous, but this was ridiculous.

Or was it?

Did Sam and Holly as sweet as they appeared to be, expect to inherit from Gregory? Had his father promised them something that he didn't know about? Just how disappointed was his father in him? Not that he didn't have good reason. He could have done more.

Much more.

Owen's cell rang breaking him out of his self-reflection. He looked at the caller ID.

Julia. Odd, over the past hours, he'd forgotten about her. Everything about his life in Chicago vanished from his mind ever since---I *kissed Angela.*

"Julia," he said answering the call as he turned away from the group who popped their heads up at the mention of his girlfriend's name. "How's it going?"

"Tell me you're on the road, Owen." Her words were biting and stern.

He had to snap himself back to reality. He had obligations. He had a career that needed attention. He had a life back there in Chicago that had been slowly retreating from him with every hour he spent on this farm. "Uh, well. A lot's been going on here. We have a new calf! Born only minutes ago. You should have been here."

"I'll pass. But I'm happy for you. But you made a promise to me, Owen. If you get in that car right now, you can just about make it."

"Right."

"I mean it, Owen."

Her terse words felt like stingers in his ear. He turned and looked at Angela and his dad. The others had gone back to tending to the calf and mother. When Owen's eyes met his dad, Gregory lowered his head and walked over to the calf. Angela stared at Owen with searching blue eyes that probed him deeper than ground penetrating radar.

No matter what had happened here, Owen's real life was in Chicago. He'd promised. He was committed. He was a man of his word.

"Right. Okay. I'll call you from the car."

He ended the call as Gregory rose from the floor where he'd been soothing the calf. He took a few steps toward Owen. "Son?"

"I should go."

"Now?"

"Yes. I've delayed long enough."

Gregory walked to Owen's side and motioned to the door. "Talk to me, son."

They went outside out of earshot of the others.

"Dad. You taught me to be a man of my word. I promised Julia I would be there for her. This is an important night for her. I have to go."

The look in his father's eyes was compassionate. It had been years since he'd seen that level of compassion in his father. He had a vision of the day he'd left the farm after they'd buried his mother. They'd been standing next to Owen's fifteen-year-old Camero that had more miles on it than his dad's thirty-year-old tractor. And that was saying something. His father had been crying for days. He wore his pain openly and didn't give a good darn if anyone saw him in tears. That was more than Owen could say for himself. He buried his heartbreak with his mother. It was in the grave. Under the ground. Never to resurrect.

That was how Owen dealt with it all.

He didn't know how else to react to the impossible except to run away.

Now, he was doing it again. Running.

But, why?

There had been no more incidents of attack, TIA's or angina. It was only Christmas that he'd be gone. He could always come back for New Year's. Couldn't he?

"You take care, Owen. Drive safely."

"I'll do my best."

Owen gave his dad a quick hug. Nothing too long or emotional.

Owen broke the hug and turned. He walked toward the house. The afternoon air was frosty. A wind picked up. The pine boughs waved at him. His eyes watered, obscuring his vision. A warm tear hit his cold cheek and turned icy.

It's just wind making my eyes water. He shoved his hands in his pockets.

Inside the barn, Angela watched Owen walk away from his father. She left the barn and stood by Gregory. "He's leaving."

"Yes, he is." Gregory went back into the barn.

Angela's eyes went from father to son. She wondered whose heart was breaking most.

* * * *

Nineteen

Angela stood quietly in the doorway to the sewing room watching Owen close up his suitcase and shut the laptop into its case. She kept her silence not to interrupt as he went to the dresser for his cell phone charger.

Just as he picked up three feathers that were lying on the top of the dresser, he raised his head and saw Angela's reflection in the dresser mirror.

"You put these here," he said in a voice she had learned was accusatory.

"I did not."

"Sure, you did."

There it was again. Disbelief.

She reached in her jacket pocket and pulled out the three feathers she'd found in the barn. "I kept mine. You never know who dropped them."

Angela smiled at him, but he leveled a stern eye on her. He purposefully laid the feathers back on the dresser. He picked up his suitcase.

"Cute. You know, Julia uses feathers in her Christmas designs. Lots of glitter, though."

"Maybe she knows that angel wings sparkle."

With a flourish, Owen dropped his cases on the bed.

"That's another thing! You're always talking like you…like you…"

"What?"

"I don't know. See Angels or something."

Her smile was radiant. She hoped he was beginning to understand. She hoped for so many things for Owen. "You could say that."

"And you're always so evasive," he bantered back.

She felt his frustration before he spoke. It reminded her of the incident in the barn. "Not when you were kissing me," she said as spirals of joy whirled through her heart.

He hung his head. "No." He looked at her as she walked across the room toward him. "I agree. Not then."

She took his hand and kissed his palm as he'd done to her.

"It was my honor to meet you, Owen. You changed my perspective about so many things."

He curled his fingers around hers and his voice lowered to a soft whisper.

"Like what?" he asked.

"I think being you is very difficult."

He inhaled deeply as if he didn't expect her observation. "You understand that?"

"I do. You are torn between your promises to both your life where you live and the life you wish you had."

He jerked his head back. "Now you're scaring me."

"Truth can do that."

Owen moved very close. Almost like a hug. She believed he wanted to kiss her. Angela held herself steady so that she did not lose her balance, or become dizzy like she did when they danced. Or like it was for her first kiss from him.

Owen's cell phone rang.

He halted.

Angela could tell he was measuring his response and actions. This point was for him a crossroads. Many humans came to these junctures of free will. What she did not realize was how quickly humans were forced to make these decisions. Even in her dimension where time did not exist, there was the avenue of contemplation and reflection. Owen had none of that.

For him it was a point of honor and obligation to answer his call.

"It's Julia. Again."

He did not look happy, Angela thought. "I know."

Angela walked to the doorway, though she did not leave. She wanted Owen to have privacy. She knew what was happening. She wanted him to know that she was here. Supporting. Adding her presence. Angelic presence.

"Owen," Julia said. "Hear me out."

"Okay."

"I've been so nuts with all this work I've been doing. I really am off, here. But amazingly, in the midst of all this turmoil, it's like I'm seeing things clearly for the first time."

"What are you saying?"

"Don't come."

"Excuse me? I didn't get that."

"I'm fine, Owen. But we are not."

Owen's chin dropped to his chest. He toed the floor. "We're not. Are we?"

"No," Julia replied. "Not for quite some time if either of us was honest. You should stay there for Christmas. You're needed there. Be there with your dad. It's the right thing to do."

"And you?"

"My gala looks to be the success I've wanted. My parents are so proud of me, Owen. Theirs is the accolade I've dreamed of. It's what I needed. For me. And the rest---I'll figure it out."

"Julia---I---Merry Christmas, Julia."

"Merriest of Christmases, Owen. I mean that," she said and hung up.

Owen stared at the cell for a long moment.

Slowly, Angela walked back into the sewing room. She didn't want to take Owen from his thoughts too quickly. This was a sacred moment in his life. Endings were as important, as divine as the beginnings.

"Your friend---she understands a great deal."

"Wish I did," he replied looking up from the phone with a pensive expression.

"You do." She walked back through the door, stopped and looked back at him over her shoulder. "Truly."

* * * * *

Angela was followed by Beau as she walked into Owen's bedroom. The late afternoon sun showered gold rays through the window. Outside, the long winter shadows spread across the snow-covered farm land, the hills and evergreens, the barn and calf hatches. Angela thought of the lovely hours she'd spent here in the timeline of Owen, Gregory, their friends, the farm animals, and the giving trees.

She looked down at Beau.

He peered up at her, and though his eyes were animal eyes, she knew he was a deep soul. He would not have been able to communicate with her the way he had if he had not been special. Superior intelligence.

"Were you waiting for me to come out of Owen's room? Its fine if you were."

"I know who you are Angel 7777."

"And you know this because you are a dog?"

"You are making a joke. No. Because they told me," Beau stated telepathically, raising his head to the ceiling.

"They do that a lot. I suppose they told you why I'm here."

"They said because of Love. I see that."

"Do you now?"

"At least I'm trying," Beau answered.

Angela walked over to the desk and began opening drawers.

"I can help. What are you looking for?"

"Kris told me I'd find them in here." She rummaged around in every drawer, and sure enough, she found charcoal drawing pencils, artist paper and colored pencils.

She sat down at the desk next to the sewing machine and began drawing. Her practice work on the cookies had aided her well in using earth tools for her artistry. But the thoughts and visions that scampered through her mind easily found their way to her hands and were illustrated in all their glory on the papers in the stack.

Beau sat at her feet and slept.

Angela continued drawing until night fall. Though it was odd, this manner of drawing, the process was a gift. Now she understood the sensations and joy that her artist recipients experienced when she sent them visions and inspirations.

Working with the divine created a magnificent flow of energy, of light and even sound, she realized as she finished one scroll and went to the next. It took long hours to manifest her Christmas present she would bestow on Owen and Gregory, but in the tedium of the heaviness of earthly time, there was contemplation, determination, choice, free will and faith. It was the faith that gave her pause.

Because she existed in the place of All That There Is, All That There Was and All That There Will Be, faith to her was the essence of an angel's nature. Angels did not question their faith.

They did not have to.

They were attached to it, in it, and existed because of it.

Faith was their nature.

From her observations, she concluded that humans had diverted their faith from the divine to the illusion of the timeline that had been created for them prior to their entrance to the earth. Their faith was based in fear.

Few found joy and love in nature.

She had been wise to volunteer for this assignment. Gregory was the epitome of a human still attached to his divine nature. He'd lived nearly his entire earthly existence on this magnificent farm. His love bloomed across every acre, in every fistful of soil that nurtured the trees. She knew because she was one with the consciousness of nature on the farm. The frozen creek that ran down the north face of the high hill, possessed a sentient beingness that Gregory understood.

Angela sensed that Sam and Holly were of the same like-mindedness as Gregory. They and their children exuded a love for the farm that was sincere.

Owen had once been of the same mind as all of them, and especially of his father. He had lost his way.

"Coercing a human to admit to their broken heart is a difficult task, Beau," she said telepathically.

Beau did not budge.

"Sleep well, my friend."

Picking up another colored pencil, she continued working. Earth time was drawing her mission to a close. She had been told she must 'awaken' Owen to his truth. If he spurned her intervention, she was not allowed to help him. Unless he asked.

Angels always answered heartfelt entreaties to bring assistance to humans, when the request was for the soul's highest good. It was too bad some humans did not believe that angels or any of the divine realms were aiding them in their successes. Too often, when the "miracle" occurred, they dismissed angelic work or worse, took credit for themselves. Either way, there was no gratitude exchanged.

She had been fortunate in her work, being a muse, an inspiration to artists. As a group they were effusive with thanksgiving. Other angels probably felt as she felt now with her work with Owen---disheartened.

Night was falling as she put down her pencil finally satisfied with her work.

Being hampered by pencils and human hands made this a task. But filled with even more love.

She rolled up each one, tied them with a ribbon and made tags that she attached to the ribbon.

"C'mon Beau. Wake up. Time for us to interrupt them."

"Do what?"

Dutifully, Beau rose and followed her out of the room, down the hall and to the Christmas tree.

Angela placed each of the rolled "scrolls" under the tree. She stood back and admired the beauty of the happy tree. "Thank you, tree, for giving your life to bring your beauty to this special day. You gave me joy." She inhaled the distinct citrus and pine scent of the conifer tree. She loved the fragrance of all the trees, but this one was special. Owen and Gregory had planted it when Owen was a child. She couldn't help imbibing her senses…

"One last time," she said telepathically.

Beau's head lifted. "Last?"

Angela started to walk away. Beau went in front of her and barricaded her from another step.

"You said 'last time.'"

"I did."

"That is because it is Christmas tomorrow. The holiday is over."

"Yes, Beau."

"I don't believe you."

"You must. I am an angel. I tell the truth. Always."

* * * * *

Twenty

Owen hauled the roasting pan out from under the stove and put it next to the sack of potatoes on the counter. Next to it were two pie pumpkins he would clean out, cut up and boil for the pumpkin pie. In the sink rested the twenty-pound fresh turkey his father had bought from the butcher in Black River. Owen had cleaned out the interior, put the giblets, liver and neck in a pot with poultry seasoning to cook. This would be the water he would use to make his mother's giblet gravy. Even now he could taste the thyme, butter and seasonings she used to make the best gravy he'd had in his life.

Earlier, he'd found his mother's old recipe box where she kept the recipes of every one of Owen's favorite cookies, pies, casseroles and vegetable dishes he loved. As he thumbed through them looking for the pumpkin pie recipe, he was surprised at how his tastes had changed.

How my life has changed.

That was what happened in life. People grew. They broadened their horizons, their goals, their ambitions. They improved. Sought knowledge.

He'd done all that, hadn't he?

Or so he thought before he came home for Christmas. It wasn't his father's heart attack that had suddenly made him question many aspects about himself. Who he was. Where he was going.

It was Angela.

A total stranger. Strange wasn't the only word for her. She could not be stranger if she had fallen from the sky. He was convinced she had been in some kind of accident that had disoriented her; caused a concussion and apparently some kind of amnesia.

He'd been a fool to allow himself to become this attracted her, but the inevitable happened. She was a goddess.

But whose goddess was she before she appeared here?

Now, the fear in the back of his mind that she might have a boyfriend or lover searching for her, gnawed at him. It didn't matter that Owen had feelings for her. That he might be falling in love with her. She had to have a prior life. It was impossible for her to simply appear on the farm as if she had been transported.

That wasn't out of the question these days. Maybe she was an alien.

Oh, that is all I need, Owen thought as he pulled a large pot out of the lower cupboard.

Owen had gone out to the herb garden that was under the kitchen window, close to the house where the hardier herbs grew even after snow falls, due to the amount of heat from the house and winter sunshine. Thyme and sage grew all winter. He cut off several springs of younger looking sage leaves. He washed them, then patted them dry with a paper towel.

Gregory was busying himself with making homemade cranberry sauce. He used a microblade to grate the rind off a fat orange. Taking the pot of cooked cranberries off the stove, Gregory stirred the orange zest into the berries. "Just like your mom used to make."

Owen watched his father. "Is that what she did? I always wondered why her cranberry sauce was so much better than any…."

Owen paused as Gregory took up the microblade again.

"Now, what are you doing?

Gregory grinned. "This is the other secret. Fresh nutmeg and a couple pinches of cinnamon." Gregory finished with the spices then he went to the liquor cabinet and withdrew a bottle.

"What now?"

"Just a touch of brandy."

Owen laughed. "Okay. I really missed this one. Did you always do this?"

"Yep. Long before you were born. I also put Cream Sherry in the creamed pearl onions."

"And I thought I had sophisticated tastes," Owen quipped.

Gregory picked up a pair of oven mitts, then looked at Owen. "Do you miss not being with your girl? That fancy party of hers is quite sophisticated, isn't it?"

Owen put his palms on the counter, tilted his head toward the window where he could see brilliant stars in the ebony sky. "Interesting." He looked at his father. "I hadn't thought about her till you mentioned her and the party."

"Guess your heart wasn't in it."

"Guess not."

Gregory took the loaf of bread he'd made out of the oven. The room filled with the smell of yeast and fresh bread. He picked up a box of instant turkey stuffing.

Owen's jaw dropped. "And what—are you doing with that?"

"It's good stuffing and cuts down on time," Gregory replied.

"Oh. No. This is *not* how you stuff a turkey."

"How would you know? When was the last time you were here to stuff a turkey?"

"Dad. Can we not go there?"

"I apologize. But I know plenty about turkeys."

Slamming his hand on his hip, Owen said, "I know more. I was in the kitchen with mom every holiday while you were…."

"In the barn working?" Gregory's eyebrow shot up.

"I didn't mean it that way. Yes. You worked hard. You still do and shouldn't. But never mind. I know how mom did it."

Gregory put the box down. "Regretfully, I don't know how she did it. "

"She put the washed sage leaves in between the breast meat and the turkey skin. Then butter the inside and the outside. When it browns in the oven, it looks like…"

"Art." Angela's voice came from the doorway.

Beau was at her feet. He padded over to his doggie bed and laid down. Watching.

Owen snapped his fingers. "Exactly, Angela! It is art."

"Sounds complicated," Gregory huffed.

Owen continued. "I stuff the turkey cavity with orange slices, quartered onions, celery and more sage." Owen put the clean and washed turkey on the buttered roasting pan and placed it in the middle of the counter top.

Beau licked his chops.

"Kris never told me all this." Gregory said.

Owen scrubbed out the kitchen sink with bleach just as his mother had instructed to clean away all chance of salmonella.

"Dad---you had a mountain of work. She did the cooking. I helped both of you."

"How nice you all worked together," Angela offered, but Gregory's face was downcast. She could not read his thoughts. She did not know if he had regrets or if Owen reminded him too much of the time when Kris was alive.

Angela knew the kind of tremendous energy it took for spirit beings to come back to loved ones on earth. Kris had been visible to Gregory several times, Angela knew. She also knew that Kris could not come not through the dimensions very often. It would be a waste of spirit. However, when sadness filled the heart of a loved one, it was difficult for the spirit being not to respond.

Angela walked over to look at the turkey. "Show me more about the way you make art," she said to Owen.

Gregory dried his hands. "I'll check on Sam. The light is still on in the barn. It's late and he should go home for the day. After all, it is Christmas Eve." Gregory went to the peg and grabbed his parka.

Beau lifted his head, got up and followed Gregory outside.

Owen looked at Angela. "He's upset."

"He misses your mother."

"I was hoping…." Owen looked at Angela.

She put her hand over his. "Deep down. He is happy you stayed."

"He doesn't act like it. And he doesn't say that, either. He never says that."

Angela peered into Owen's eyes. "Do you?"

He dropped his chin. "I thought I did." He glanced up at her.

Angela continued to look at him unwavering.

He frowned. "Okay," he said. "Maybe I didn't. Maybe I should. But seriously, would it make a difference? Really?"

"Test it."

"I don't know."

Angel shook her head at him. He was as stubborn as a mountain that would not move on her command. She took out a bowl from the cabinet, went to the refrigerator and withdrew a bowl of fresh farm eggs. She opened the blue and white china sugar canister.

Beating the eggs and sugar with a whisk, she smiled at Owen.

"Okay. So now you don't like my turkey either?"

Angela continued beating the eggs. "I would never eat a creature. Like one of your cows. They are so friendly and giving."

Owen looked at the turkey. Compassion riddled him. "I see your point. "What are you making?"

"Christmas cake. I saw it on the holographic box."

"Box?"

"Near the Christmas tree."

"Ah!" His head reared back with understanding. "Television."

"I like demonstrations." She picked up the bottle of French vanilla. She whisked a small amount into the mixture. "You didn't answer my question."

Quirking the corner of his mouth, he answered, "Evasion. One of my strong suits."

She nodded. "It is. You accused me of being just that. All I did was copy your mannerisms."

His eyes flew wide. "Why would you do that? Now, I'm a study model?"

"Aren't all humans study models? I find them very complicated. Their emotions fly around in their hearts like leaves in a whirlwind."

"You talk like you're not human," he said accusingly.

"And that confuses you?"

"Yes. No." He took a deep breath for courage and asked the question that had been haunting him. "Are you an alien?"

"Goodness no." She beat the eggs with more force and added flour.

"Good to know. It wouldn't have surprised me if you were," he replied. "I guess right now my emotions truly are all over the place."

"They are. But why, Owen?"

"For so long, I've felt the pressure of my career. I have a talent for future planning so that people don't have to struggle like my dad."

Angela stopped whipping the cake mixture. "He's not struggling."

"Sure, he is. He's stressed over the farm. It's not making money. I do his taxes for him. I know."

"What do you know?" She pressed.

"He's down to less than one hundred cows. That's half of what we used to have. Revenues have plummeted like most dairy farms. It costs a lot to pay Sam and Holly. That bites into his income."

"And you think money is the reason his heart is failing?"

"I do."

"It's not."

Angela picked up the flour and added the last amount.

Raking his hair in frustration, he barked, "And what would you, a stranger, know about us?"

Angela wiped her hands on a towel. "I know that you use your work as an excuse not to admit that one thing that will save you both."

"And what's that?"

"That you love your father."

"He knows that."

"Does he? How exactly have you shown him?"

Owen took the towel from Angela, wiped his hands, and put it down. "We're done here."

Owen stalked out of the kitchen.

Angela lifted her eyes to the ceiling. "Is it done?" She waited for heaven's answer. Dead silence communicated itself well.

*****

Twenty-One

Gregory stood at the window looking out on the full moon and the snow-covered hills and pastures of his farm. Though he wore his heaviest flannel pajamas, tonight it wasn't enough. He felt cold inside his bones to the top layers of his flesh. As he shrugged on a sweater, his left arm blazed with a red hot poker-like pain. It nearly brought him to his knees. Leaning on the big chair near the window, he bent over and steadied himself.

"It will pass. It will pass."

Beau rested on a rag rug near the bed, watching Gregory.

Finally, just as he knew it would, the pain passed. He could breathe. The stricture in his chest eased. He would fight this pain with his will and his might. He'd been a strong man of body, mind and will all his life. None of it had left him.

He had his wits about him.

Breathing deeply, he took a step and then another toward the bed. On the nightstand next to the bed was a framed photo of Kris. It had been taken on their honeymoon, many years ago. She was wearing the same bell-bottom jeans and blouse she wore now when she came to him. He knew it was only her spirit talking to him. He wasn't quite sure how she could be in heaven and be with him at the same time.

Maybe she traveled to earth on a star. Or a microwave. He didn't care. He was grateful that she came.

"They say that missing someone you loved is harder at the holidays."

Beau raised his head, listening.

"But that's not true."

"It's not?" Beau asked allowing his telepathic thoughts to come through the frequencies to Gregory for the first time.

"Every day is hard," Gregory sighed.

Gregory straightened, turned away from Kris' picture and looked at Beau. "Did you just talk to me? Or was that my thoughts?"

"That was me."

"I must be losing my mind."

Gregory looked to the window where moonbeams moved out from under a cloud and showered his room in silver light. In the light bath, Kris appeared to him.

She sat on the bed. "No, you're not, Sweetheart."

"Then what is it?" Gregory asked.

"You are seeing between the worlds. You've been seeing me and your parents."

"Oh," he pressed his palm to his forehead. "Now, I'm just nuts."

He fell back on the pillow and when he looked back, Kris had vanished. He knew she was a figment of his imagination. It was Christmas. He was lonely. He missed her so much it hurt inside.

Then again, maybe this was his miracle. Maybe this was all there was.

"Anymore---I don't even know what to wish for."

Gregory closed his eyes was instantly asleep.

* * * * *

Angela sat by the Christmas tree thinking that the tree grew more lovely with every passing minute. Or perhaps it was the magic that was Christmas all over the world. The songs and the prayers on Christmas rushed to the upper dimensions and planes carrying love and hope, joy and gratitude as no other day of the earth year did.

Rising to the nine-hundred-sixty-three frequency of her home, heaven, the human voices held a resonance that no other planetary race ever obtained. Humans were the bravest and most courageous of souls to endure the fierce density of earth. Angela had learned that truism in class.

To be on earth, to be part of this existence and to interact with humans who endeavored to do the right thing; sought to be kind and help the planet, the animals and humanity, was an overwhelming responsibility and task.

The dark polarity had ruled the underbelly of earth from ancient times. It's sway on human consciousness caused Angela to increase her prayers and petitions for the earth.

She had been exactly what she had never sought. She was the Fool Angel. She had come to earth believing she would triumph.

She had failed.

She raised her eyes to the star on top of the tree. "I wish...."

Owen walked in to the living room. "I'm sorry."

His voice was low and soft. The apology came from his heart. When she looked at him, his hands were in his pockets. Regret sat heavily on his lips.

"I accept," she said noticing how his aura brightened a bit.

"He makes me crazy you know."

"Why?"

"Because I've urged him for years to make some changes that would save the farm."

"Changes?"

"Yes," he replied coming around the sofa to sit beside her. Again, she noticed how his vibration heightened and an air of anticipation fluttered out his breath as he began to speak. What he was about to say meant a great deal to him. He'd thought about his father more than he was admitting, maybe even to himself. "I have a client who wants to start up a new cheese manufacturing company. His grandfather was in the cheese business, eons ago. It's a perfect fit for dad."

"Your father doesn't want this?"

"He won't even listen to me. I think it's because it's my idea and not his."

"He does not truly think that. Does he?" She touched his hand. "If he does, your father disappoints me."

His eyes met hers.

Again, a sensation of warmth raced through her body right to her middle. She put her hand on her stomach. Without forcing the movement with her mind, her hand covered her heart. She felt his emotions strongly in her heart.

Glancing down, he saw her movement. "I'm sorry, again. I shouldn't take my frustrations out on you."

"And your grief?"

"Grief? Over what?"

Oddly, her mouth was dry so that her tongue would not move to communicate. Why was it difficult for her to say this? "Over the loss of your friend," she finally muddled out the words.

"Julia?" He inhaled as her thoughts resonated. "The truth is, we've been drifting apart for some time."

"So, it's not a deep loss," she surmised.

"Not as much as I'd thought," he said looking down at her hand that was still resting on his. He curled his fingers around hers.

"It's not like what losing your father would be to you?" She asked.

Owen jerked back as if her words had been a blast of wind. His eyes were wide. She had shocked him.

"But---I didn't lose him. He's okay now."

"Is he?"

Owen shook his head as if to negate her thought and kill the words. The warmth from his hands turned cold as fear raced through his body. As an angel, she had not experienced fear. She was protected by divine love and her faith, but that did not exempt her from feeling his fear. Compassion filled her as she sent the highest frequencies of love to his aura and then deeper into his heart to abolish the fear.

This moment had been her most profound revelation while on earth. In her heaven, she had heard prayers from humans when they had communicated that they were fear-filled that their work would not be accepted by others, or could be exchanged for abundance in its many forms. She had never felt a human's body alter its normal regulatory systems due to an emotion and certainly not at the instant of its pitch or fall.

Again, her awareness of the density of the earth dimension, its vagaries, and the impact of negative forces on a positive human was illuminated. She had gained a great deal of knowledge and with it an empathy that she would carry back with her when this mission was completed.

"Don't say that," he said entreatingly.

"You're frightened."

"I can't let myself think it," he gasped and took his hand from hers. He placed both hands over his eyes and swiped his face. "If I go there, it might happen and that's the impossible."

"You should tell him these things," she said.

"Maybe," he sighed. "Not that it would do any good. He doesn't respect me...or my choices."

Putting her hand on his shoulder, she leaned forward, peering into his eyes. She still hoped she could convince him. "I think he does."

"Then why is he so---so—"

"Irascible?"

"YES!" Owen threw his hands in the air.

Angela withdrew her hand and started to rise. Owen took her hand.

"Wait. Where are you going?"

"To ask him why he is this way," she said.

Owen laughed. "You are something else. Nothing stops you."

"This has been said about me."

"Really? Who said that?"

"My, er---friends. They said my curiosity..."

"Would kill a cat?" He chuckled.

"I've not heard that said before," she replied.

Owen shot her a quizzical look. "It's a pretty common phrase around here. This country, I mean. Maybe you are from Canada."

"Where is that?"

Owen slapped his forehead. "Seriously? You don't know where Canada is?"

He'd trapped her again with his tricks and questions. He was ever curious about her past. And relentless even when he wasn't purposeful. "I haven't been to Canada. Have you?"

"Uh, no, actually."

She stood up. He reached for her hand.

"Please, Angela, don't."

"You don't want to know why he's this way?"

He lowered his eyes as she sat back down. "I do know. He is lost without my mom. Just don't leave. Okay?"

"Why not?" she asked aware that this time she was the one doing the probing.

She saw entreaty in his eyes as he looked at her. "I like your company."

"I like yours," she replied. She held his gaze for a long moment. There was more he wanted to say. She could feel his words and thoughts, but she could not download them properly without telepathy.

"You know," he began. "I never spent time with Julia like I do with you."

"How did the time pass for you if not sharing thoughts?"

Looking down, he said, "Well, you certainly put my relationship with her in perspective. I guess that was the problem. We did things. There was always a party, or a function. The symphony. A dinner at her father's in-town condo. Another business meeting with her father where she wanted to garner me another client."

He paused reflectively. "It was always about the trajectory."

"The trajectory?"

"The upward rise she wanted for our lives. Presumably before we would marry, though I never brought up marriage. I knew it was on her mind."

"But not on yours?"

"Deep down it wasn't right for me. And I guess not for her, either. You know, even with all that we did with her parents, I never got the feeling of 'family' with her. She was the trophy child for them. She lived her life to perform for them."

"And you aren't doing the same?"

Owen fell back on the sofa and stared hard at Angela. "Am I?"

She felt his shock with this revelation. He hadn't reflected deeply enough about himself.

"You performed for your mother," Angela said. "You thought that's what she wanted for you. Think back to your graduation party from the University. You said she told you she was proud of you. But she died before she could say more of what she wanted for you. When she left, the imprint of her pride on your soul has been your North Star. Your guide."

Leaning forward, he stared into contemplative space. The silence was long and pregnant as he explored the impact of Angela's words.

"My God, I have done just that. But if she had lived, what would she have said?" He whispered the question as if not expecting a response.

"Be happy, Owen." Angela had no idea her voice had sounded different to Owen. It was Kris's voice, tone, and reflection that he heard.

Owen jerked as if his consciousness had shot back into his body. His eyes latched onto hers. "It's the craziest thing. I feel almost as if she's here with us now."

"It is possible."

"Not really."

Angela smiled compassionately. "Christmas miracles."

"Yes," he replied turning his gaze to the Christmas tree, still contemplative.

Angela looked at the tree as well. "I like your Christmas here."

"You do?" he asked. "Is it so different than yours?" He finally looked at her.

"It is. You have so many pleasures. Cookies and the dinner for tomorrow. Mary's laughter. Holly's sigh when she looks at her children."

Nodding, he replied, "Those are special. Hmm. And don't forget my cocoa," he chuckled.

"Yes. Cocoa."

He brightened and rose. "I should make us some. And on Christmas Eve ----"

He took two candy canes off the tree and continued. "We add the peppermint stick."

Owen held out his hand to Angela as she stood next to him. She could not take her eyes from his and he was reluctant to end the moment. The love that emanated from his heart was not only warm, but she could see the pink light and hear the angelic humming sound it created as he sent the vibration to her heart. The sensation was one of embracing without his arms around her.

She took the candy cane from his hand and said, "Sharing. Is special."

Owen hesitated. "Angela, why won't you tell me where you're from?"

"You won't believe me," she replied knowing that Truth was the path to Authenticity. Owen was now on that path. Authenticity for a human was an evolved frequency eclipsing love. An authentic life embraced unconditional love and truth. Few humans reached that level of higher consciousness. She had hope for Owen.

"Angela, I'll believe what you tell me. I want to know everything about you."

At that moment, Angela glanced out the window to the night sky and the glittering stars. One particular star shone brighter than the others. It grew larger and she realized it was moving toward the house. To her.

"Owen, you'll know everything---soon."

He put his arm around her, sincerity filling his eyes. "I want to know now."

She glanced out the window. The star moved closer.

"After the cocoa," she smiled.

His smile covered his face. "Good. Yes."

Owen kissed her cheek, lingering for a long moment. "You still smell like roses. Strong, beautiful roses." He dropped his arm and went to the kitchen.

Angela walked over to the window.

The star moved closer spinning rainbow-colored lights in an ever-increasing orb around it.

* * * * *

Twenty-Two

While Owen made the hot cocoa, Angela found a long shawl in the hall closet. She went to the back porch where she could watch the star as it grew in power and brilliance. She could hear its resonance; the music of her home.

"It's time," she relayed telepathically to the energy being of light that was the star.

"Nearly midnight," the orb sent the message telepathically. "Time to complete your mission."

"What if I fail?"

"Are you refusing?"

"No. Never that," she relayed emphatically. Honor and her vow were sacred to her.

"Why do you hesitate?"

"My perspective has changed," she relayed.

"Noted. You have increased empathy."

"And something else. I think it's my heart."

Angela glanced at the kitchen window. Inside, Owen was floating marshmallows on the top of the cocoa. His face was filled with anticipation and joy. She had not seen this level of happiness in him since she came to earth.

She believed he had come to love her. Realizations about himself were many now.

At this joyous juncture in his path, she was about to deliver the greatest heartbreak of his life.

She was learning lessons as well. Angels had the strength of a thousand dragons. She would not shirk her vow. She was an angel of the higher celestial realms. This mission was entrusted to her. Her Superior had faith in her.

"Here we go!" He said cheerfully as he walked out of the kitchen onto the porch.

Though the star was pulsating beams of violet, blue, orange, pink, green and red, Angela realized that Owen didn't see the star. It was cloaked to humans.

He handed her a mug and clinked his with hers. "Merry Christmas, Angela."

He sipped his cocoa.

Angela did not. The moment was heavy on her heart. She endured a sinking vibration that she realized was the emotion Owen would feel when she finished her mission.

"What's wrong?" he asked.

"You were right. Leaving causes a great pain...in here." She placed her hand over her heart.

He slipped his arm around her shoulder. "I told you. I figured it out. I'm meeting with my clients through Zoom. It's not all that far to drive to Chicago if I need. I can stay here with dad---"

She interrupted. "No, Owen you don't understand."

Looking back at the hilltop, the rainbow orb had settled at the apex. It sparkled. It beckoned.

The magnetic pull from the orb was powerful and sent a chill over Angela.

"You're cold," Owen observed and pulled the shawl up to cover the back of her neck.

She drank the cocoa thinking how much she would miss this simple pleasure.

Owen pulled her close into almost a hug.

This warmth she would never forget.

"You're freezing. We should go inside," he said.

Owen put their mugs on the railing and drew her close for a kiss. As endearing and love-filled as his lips were, Angela's heartstrings were plucked with sadness.

"I wish you trusted me enough to tell me about yourself. Or is it that you still don't remember your life? I mean what if you had a husband? A family?"

"No husband. No children. Only me. Owen. I am not like you. I am without family."

"Whew," he chuckled. "I was worried because I'm sure I'm falling in love with you."

He quickly pulled her close for a tight hug, laughing lightly. Continuing, he said, "You know, I don't care where you're from or what career you have, other than your art, which is fantastic."

"It's a gift and I honor it."

"I'm glad."

He kissed her forehead.

Angela hugged him back. "I'll miss this. I'll miss everything," she whispered and shivered again.

Owen pulled back. "Don't talk like that. Seriously, let's go inside."

Shaking her head, she glanced at the sky. At the orb. "I like to be outside at midnight on Christmas Eve."

"Is that a tradition of yours?"

"Yes. That is it. A tradition."

Owen glanced at his watch. "Still twenty-one more minutes. I better get you more cocoa."

"Thank you. I'd like that."

Angela watched Owen take the mug and go inside. He turned on the stove to heat up the cocoa. She turned toward the orb.

"I hear you," she said dropping the shawl.

She walked down the steps and across the backyard, toward the high hill.

The orb flashed its rainbow light brightly, bathing the hill and farm in sparkling multi-colored rays.

* * * * *

Gregory was awakened by the bright rainbow lights cascading through the window.

"What in the world?"

Beau woke up. Turned his head toward the light coming through the window and said telepathically, "It's time."

Though groggy, Gregory rose from the bed, put on his robe and slippers and leaving his parka on the chair, he walked like a somnambulist out of his room with Beau by his side.

He went to the living room where he saw the transparent spirits of Kris, David and Penny sitting on the sofa. They said nothing, but smiled as he opened the front door and went outside. He didn't notice that Kris and his parents followed him. He walked around the house to the back yard and saw Angela walking up the hill.

"Where is she going, Beau?"

Looking up, the magnificent lights at the top of the hill grew larger and brighter.

* * * * *

Angela was only half way up the hill when the "change" erupted. Kris's clothes fell away and she was dressed in her white gown, gold wing clips and gold belt. The human body that had been her encasement, transformed. She was lighter. Her energy was profound. She had almost forgotten the radiance her angelic being exuded. The light from the orb increased as waves of light undulated toward her and around her with unconditional love. The embrace was not unlike that of being human and wrapped in Owen's arms.

By the time she floated to the very top of the hill, her wings had fanned to their normal width. They glowed with golden light that on earth resonated with an intensity that was her natural vibration. On earth, as they spread wider, they created a sweet pitched sound much like her own voice when she sang for the crowd at the Black River Barn.

Her wings rivaled the silver beams from the full moon. The stars glittered in the night sky and the rainbow orb held its luminescence.

Gregory's feet felt like lead as he struggled up the hill, but the vision of Angela as an angel was magnetic. He could not take his eyes from the majesty of the moment. It was as if a star had come to earth and posited itself on his hill.

His breath was short and difficult to draw with each step.

Pain seared a hot trail across his chest. Then across his back and down his arm. He stumbled and fell.

Angela watched Gregory and Beau. "Come to me, Gregory. You can make it."

Pushing his weakened body, Gregory was empowered by Angela's words. She was blinding in her resplendence. Surely, this wasn't the young woman who'd been living in his house these past few days. Yet. By some miracle, she had done just that. He couldn't take his eyes off her.

"I'll do it. I'll make it."

"Yes," she encouraged. "I believe in you."

He paused for a moment. "From the first day I found you, in my heart, I felt you were an angel."

"Yes. You did."

* * * * *

Owen turned on the kitchen faucet to clean out the mugs. Turning off the water, he looked up, expecting to see Angela on the porch waiting for him. Instead, he winced as brilliant rainbow lights shone in his face. He put up his palm to shield his eyes.

"What?"

The lights were strong and formed a circle around a white center that twinkled or pulsed like a star. He rushed out the door and onto the porch. "What's going on?" He looked around the porch and saw the shawl on the floor. He picked it up and as he straightened, he saw his father, dressed in his robe and slippers walking, stumbling up the hill in the distance. Beau followed his father.

"Holy---- Dad! Dad!"

He started down the porch steps and halted. Illuminated by the orb lights was the silhouette of an expanse of wings that had to be ten to fifteen feet across. Then he saw her.

She was dressed just as she had been the night of the winter solstice when he and his father had found Angela on the hill. The white gown with gold clips on her shoulders and a gold belt.

Angela is an angel.

Truth registered shock, which devolved further to denial.

Impossible. A fantasy.

He wasn't sure he had ever believed in angels. Yet here he and his father had been living with one. And unbelievably, he'd fallen in love with her.

Mortals falling for goddesses. He knew this story. He'd read every Greek myth his college professor had required. But those were dramas, illustrations of truth. Not *the truth.*

But this episode he'd just lived proved he had been wrong all his life.

Here, in front of his eyes was Angela revealing that her essence was divine.

His father was over half-way up the hill. Angela or the angel was waiting for him.

Was this what she meant when she said she was leaving?

And why was his father struggling to get to her?

Fear crept through his body, turning his stomach to ice. The terror of reality hit him. "Dad! Dad! Don't go!"

Angela is the angel of death.

Owen watched as his father stumbled again, but his iron will did not fail him. Gregory rose. The light around Angela glowed like a hundred bonfires. He was stunned that no one else saw it. There were no sirens from a neighbor's 911 call. No firetrucks or ambulance. No evidence that anyone except he and his father saw the lights. Saw the Angel.

This is a nightmare.

No. He was absolutely in his awake consciousness.

Angela looked down as Gregory reached her feet. He could not breathe. This time when he fell, he did not get up. He grabbed his chest and was barely able to say, "This is why you came."

"Time to go home," Angela replied.

Owen raced to the top of the hill. "Dad! Please!"

He rushed over to his father and fell to his knees beside him. "Dad."

Gregory looked up at Owen, his lips quivering, he took a last breath. He never exhaled.

Owen lifted his father close to his chest. Tears burned paths down his cheeks. He was out of breath himself, but not from running. A strange constriction in his chest, near his heart tightened and squeezed. He closed his eyes to stop the tears, but they came in torrents.

He looked up at Angela. "Don't take him! Please."

"This is my mission," Angela replied holding out her arms to take Gregory.

A fiery courage filled Owen as he pulled his father closer. He gathered his body to him with the vain hope that he could will Gregory to life; infuse his dad with his own will. "I won't let you take him!"

Angela's wings raised high above her back, ready to take flight.

Owen saw it. Terror struck him like an icy glacier. Hard. Cold. Permanent.

She looked at Owen. "Why not, Owen?"

Her words were loud and echoed in the frosty night air around them like circling banshees.

"Because I love him! I love him!" Owen shouted through tears.

Angela smiled. Soft. Compassionate. Unconditionally. "That's all I wanted to hear."

Owen looked into Gregory's ashen face as the rainbow lights showered father and son. The lights flashed above them and spread out over the sky like the Aurora Borealis Owen had been searching for.

Gregory's eyelids fluttered. His top lip twitched.

Owen sucked in his breath over the miracle taking place in his arms.

"I love you, Dad. I love you," he said repeatedly.

Gregory's eyes were reluctant to open. His consciousness was slow to return. "I---I love you, Owen."

Owen hugged his father again. He couldn't get close enough. "I've always loved you. I always will."

The pulsating rainbow lights swept back to an orb that circled around the trio on the hill until it formed a small ball. As if sucked into a black hole, the orb vanished.

"Angela," Owen said as he and Gregory watched the spectacle.

Without another word, the radiant light around Angela faded. Her wings folded around her body and she vanished.

Beau raced up to the place where Angela had been and sniffed the vacant ground. He whimpered. Then he sauntered over to Owen and Gregory.

Gregory coughed and gulped the air. Finally, his eyes opened completely. He looked up at Owen who was still holding him.

"Dad? Dad? How...."

"Owen. I had the most magical and wonderful dream."

"It wasn't a dream," Owen replied looking at the dark hill. Slowly, Gregory sat up.

"How do you feel?" Owen touched his father's cheek that was pink and healthy.

"I'm fine."

"But your heart. You were short of breath climbing the hill." Owen helped him to his feet.

"This little hill? No way."

Owen looked over again at the top of the hill. "She's gone."

"Who?"

"Angela."

Gregory scratched his head. "Angela. I remember. So, not a dream?"

"No, Dad. None of it was a dream," Owen answered.

Owen, glanced around and watched Beau as he still sniffed the ground. "Then where did she go?"

"Heaven. This time she's really gone. And she won't be coming back." Owen's smile was small as he fought the lump of emotion in his throat. "But we have each other."

"We do," Gregory smiled and hugged his son. "Merry Christmas, son. I love you."

"Dad---that's all I wanted to hear."

* * * * *

Twenty-Three

Fluffy snowflakes fell like white angel feathers on the farm just as Sam, Holly, Mary and Joe opened their gifts from Gregory and Owen. Colored tissue paper fluttered on top of red and green bows. There was a new bandana for Beau. Homemade chocolate fudge for Owen and a knitted winter scarf Holly had made for Gregory. Gregory had purchased new bicycle horns, lights and reflectors for both the kids. Owen's parka for his father had not arrived on time due to the weather, he was told in an email from the department store. He was given a gift certificate for the inconvenience that he promptly gave to Mary and Joe for them to spend. On line.

It was Mary's job, being the youngest and smallest to scamper under the tree to retrieve any remaining gifts.

She backed out from under the tree and announced, "Look what I found!" She held all the rolled up "scrolls" close to her chest as she read off the names.

As they each unrolled Angela's colored pencil portraits of themselves, they gasped almost in unison.

"These are uncanny likenesses," Holly remarked.

"Beautiful," Sam said.

Owen felt tears well in his eyes. In the past twelve hours he hadn't been this emotional since… *Mom died.*

"She was real," Owen's words spoken under breath were heard by everyone.

Gregory stared long at the portrait. "Who's to say what's real and what isn't?"

Holly held her portrait to the light. "Sometimes I think our world is the dream and her world is real."

Sam cut in. "I hope not! I'm loving my dream with you!" He leaned over and kissed his wife lovingly.

Watching Sam and Holly's happiness bit into Owen's heart. He was happy for them, but suddenly, he found himself in love for the first time in his life. With an angel. A non-human.

He had no idea how he would mend his broken heart. It had taken an angel from heaven to help him through the grief of losing his mother and to repair the rift that he had made with his father. On so many levels, Owen felt the fool.

In other ways, he felt more blessed than a human had a right to be.

He didn't know what was so special about himself or his father that called heaven to smile on him, but it had. He had experienced something grand, awesome, and impossible. For a short time, he had a moment of happiness that would have to last the rest of his life.

He hadn't done anything to earn such magic, but perhaps that was the way it was supposed to happen. Heaven had it's own rules. That was for sure.

Everything on the farm would remind him of Angela.

Beau rose from the warm floor by the fireplace and nuzzled Owen. Owen put his hand on Beau's head. "You miss her, too."

Beau whimpered.

Ding. Ding.

"Doorbell!" Mary shouted starting to rise.

Owen stopped her with his hand on her shoulder. "You play with your new toys. I'll get it."

They had all been so busy opening gifts and having fun, that no one had paid attention to the fact that the snow had piled up a great deal outside. As Owen opened the door, he was hit with a blast of strong wind.

Half expecting the department store delivery of his dad's new parka, Owen was quite surprised to see a young, beautiful woman, wearing a knit hat, stylish parka, jeans, leather boots and a scarf over half her face. A snow had fallen on her hat, shoulders and long eyelashes.

"Hi!" she waved jauntily.

Before Owen could respond, she barreled into her explanation.

"I hate to bother you on Christmas Day, but my cell is out of charge. I forgot my car charger and stupid me, I didn't fill up when I left Black River. I was so excited to get home for Christmas—you know how that goes, right? So, bottom line to my tragic story is my car is dead. I'm late and well, can I use your phone?" She hadn't taken a single breath.

She pulled down her scarf and whipped off her knit hat revealing dark, thick, chin length hair that glistened even under grey snow-filled skies.

Owen blinked.

Not possible.

The woman was the spitting image of Angela, but with dark hair. Her deep sky-blue eyes held the same intensity and vitality he'd seen each and every time he'd looked at Angela.

He was tongue-tied. "You have family?"

"Yeah. Yeah. In Madison. My sister's having a baby any minute. Her third and trust me on this one, my brothers are never gonna let me live this one down. Not being there for all the excitement." She glanced behind her. "Wow. Some storm, huh? I swear it's snowed a foot while I walked up your drive."

"Oh, my gosh!" Owen said, glancing, but only momentarily behind her to see the snow accumulating in the drive. "I'm sorry. Come in. Come in."

"Thanks."

She stepped inside, but had not taken her eyes from Owen. Her smile was warm as she shook off the snow in her hair.

"You're from Madison?" He asked still astounded that this woman showed up on his doorstep looking uncannily like Angela.

"All my life," she rattled. "Guess you wanna know what I'm doing here in Black River. On Christmas Day, no less. Huh? Well, I'll tell ya. I just interviewed yesterday for the new position as the Elementary School Art Teacher and for the Disabled Children's Mentor Program. Have you heard about that?"

"Uh, yeah. Sure. We all have. Congratulations. I mean. That's cool. Interviews are tough." Owen stuttered still taken aback by how much this woman even sounded like Angela.

"Don't I know it. I'm not bonkers about them. I'll tell ya."

"Due to…" Owen offered.

"I talk too much. Babble. You know?"

"I noticed," he laughed.

"Sorry." Her apology wasn't in the least sheepish.

"No! I…love it," he said sincerely. Angela could hardly speak when she arrived. It made sense now. He wouldn't understand angelic language in the least.

But this woman was a delight to him.

Mary and Joe had been eavesdropping and they slowly moved away from the tree and toward the door. Mary couldn't take the excitement any longer.

"You're going to teach at my school?" She bounced up and down in her new lighted sneakers.

"Black River Elementary?"

"Yeah," Mary answered.

"I sure am and I'm looking forward to every minute." She looked at Owen.

It wasn't just the color of her eyes that captured him, but the openness of her heart that invited him in that made him breathless.

She continued babbling. "I went to University of Wisconsin. Loved it there. I would have stayed on to complete my masters, but my mama got sick and I had to go home and help my dad. Oh, she's right as rain, now. God love her. After all what would we ever do without her pecan pie and homemade whipped cream at Christmas. We always whip our own. Must be a Wisconsin thing, don't ya think? Oh, sorry, I got off- track. What I meant to tell you was that I graduated in Art History and studied Renaissance Masters paintings on the side."

He nearly howled; he was so awed. "Of course, you did." He looked around. "Let me take your coat. The phone is in the kitchen but first you should meet my family."

He stepped behind her and helped her with her coat. The very strong rose essence filled the space between them. It wasn't like the soft drift of Angela's rose. This was strong and unmistakable. Just like her personality.

Untwirling the neck scarf, she asked, "These your kids?"

"No. I borrow them," he joked.

She laughed and when she did it was like tinkling music. Angelic music, he thought.

She took a few steps into the living and room and stopped cold. "That is the most incredible tree ever! Ever, I tell ya!"

"I think so."

"I could look at it forever," she said winsomely turning back to Owen.

Forever.

She had a way of looking at him as if he was the only man on earth. It sent tingles down his spine and put a smile on his face.

She was the familiarity of Angela, but so much more.

"My favorite word—forever," he said aloud, still half breathless.

She looked at Owen with eyes that went straight to his heart. "Mine, too."

"I'm Owen, by the way. This is my dad, Gregory Michaels."

Gregory rose easily. No twinges. No pain. He felt thirty years younger. He held out his hand. "Nice to meet you."

"Angie Starr," she said. "No relation to Bart Starr." Her laugh was lilting, and filled with genuine delight.

Owen's surprise had upgraded to awe. He took a step back where his eyes met his father's beaming face. He mouthed, "Angie? Angel?"

Gregory nodded knowingly as Owen noticed Holly slipping a glance to Sam. The kids were ear to ear grins.

"Uh, Angie. These are our dear friends, Holly and Sam Kane."

Holly immediately closed the distance between them and hugged Angie. "Merry Christmas, Angie. I just know you're a hugger."

"I am! Thanks for that," Angie smiled. "My mama always says you can tell a lot about a person in the way they hug. Of course, my whole family is huggers. My daddy says nobody in the family ever met a stranger," she giggled.

Sam laughed. "Well, you met your match with my Holly."

Owen cocked his head. "Really? You never hugged me." His voice held an unintended mournful ring.

Holly's eyebrow shot up. "Why Owen, you weren't the hugging type. But I think something has changed." She threw open her arms and hugged Owen. "Merry Christmas, Owen."

"Wow. I like that," he replied truthfully. "Merry Christmas, Holly."

"So," Sam said. "You need some help with the car? I have a couple gallons of gas next door. That would get you back to town and a gas station."

Gregory looked out the wide living room window. The wind mysteriously and furiously blew snow against the window pane. "I wouldn't advise anyone venturing into that white out."

The kids raced to the window. "Wow!" Joe said. "It's a real blizzard."

"And all of a sudden, too," Mary added.

"I have to tell my family I'll be late for everything. Even Christmas dinner."

Gregory clapped his hands together. "Have dinner with us. I have a twenty-pound turkey."

Angie sniffed the aromas from the kitchen. "I couldn't intrude. Wow. That sure smells good. Is that sage?"

"It is," Owen said proudly. "And the oranges I put in the turkey."

"I use apples," Angie said. "But this smells even better. I'll have to try it. I just love to cook."

"So, you're not vegetarian?" Owen asked moving a step closer to Angie.

"Goodness, no. I tried it once and I tell ya, I got sick. Yep. Blood count went down like a rock falling off a cliff. Doctor said I had the wrong blood type for being vegan or vegetarian.

Not that I don't like my veggies. I love them. I grow my own, you know. Well, I guess when I move, I'll have to find a house to rent with a yard big enough for vegies and an herb garden. Can't live without herbs. Nothing like home grown thyme, rosemary, and sage. Mint, too. I love mint. How about you, Owen?"

He didn't hear a word she said. He was enraptured with her almost as totally as he had been with Angela. Or was this, Angela? How could he ever tell? She didn't have wings. He checked when he took her coat. Normal human back.

What did that say about his experience? Now he was checking strangers out to see if they were human or non-human. Truly. His perspective on life had been blown.

"Owen?" Angie waited for his answer.

Her eyes were locked onto his and he didn't want to look at anyone else either. "Uh, yeah. I cook a lot when I'm here."

"You just visiting, then?"

"Actually," he glanced at his father. "I'm moving back home. Permanently."

"That's—wonderful. Then. I'll see you when I move right after the first of the year."

"I hope so."

Gregory looked at Sam. "Put another log on the fire, Sam. I'll get the champagne. This calls for a toast. We have a new friend in Black River."

As Gregory went into the kitchen and returned with glasses and an opened bottle of champagne, Holly helped him pour. Owen handed Angie a glass of champagne and they walked over to the Christmas tree.

"It's so beautiful." Angie touched an old popsicle stick ornament. "We used to make these at home."

"The older ornaments my mom and I made. The newer ones were made by a recent friend. But she went away."

"I guess we have the same taste in what a real Christmas tree should be, huh?" Her eyes drifted back to him and captured him more forcefully than Angela ever had. He realized now that Angela had always known she would be leaving. She had not come here to stay.

Who was to say if this was a coincidence, serendipity or if this Angie was heaven sent by Angela as his Christmas miracle? Whatever it was, he was not going to let it pass him by.

He clinked his glass to hers. "Merry Christmas, Angie."

"Merry Christmas, Owen," she replied not taking her eyes from his as she took a sip of the champagne.

"Oh gosh," he said, feeling the comfortable heart connection with Angie. Owen felt his smile start in his heart before it broke loose on his face. "I forgot. I need to show you the phone."

"Phone? Oh, yeah." Her smile radiated in her beautiful face. "Sure. But I have time."

Owen held his breath. "How much?"

When she smiled a beam of rainbow-colored lights glittered around the room.

"All the time in the world."

THE END

www.ingramcontent.com/pod-product-compliance
Lightning Source LLC
LaVergne TN
LVHW021804060526
838201LV00058B/3228